# ASH ON AN OLD MAN'S SLEEVE

*Also by Francis King*

# ASH ON AN
# OLD MAN'S SLEEVE

## Francis King

Constable · London

First published in Great Britain 1996
by Constable and Company Limited
3 The Lanchesters, 162 Fulham Palace Road
London W6 9ER
Copyright © Francis King 1996
The right of Francis King to be identified as author of this work
has been asserted by him in accordance with the Copyright,
Designs and Patents Act 1988
ISBN 0 09 475590 6
Set in Linotron Palatino 11pt by CentraCet Ltd, Cambridge
Printed in Great Britain by St Edmundsbury Press Ltd
Bury St Edmunds, Suffolk

A CIP catalogue record of this book is available
from the British Library

FOR

JONATHAN FRYER

# 1

*Surprise me!*

I couldn't. To surprise others is something that the old can rarely do. Then, that night, newly dumped in an alien city, I achieved something even more difficult for the old: I surprised myself.

I was alone because, on the previous day, I had received a telephone call from my travelling companion to tell me, in a voice quavering with a mixture of weakness and apprehension, that it was such a bore, they had had to cart him off to the Princess Grace; his prostate was playing up, it looked as if he was once again due for the chop; he was terribly, terribly sorry to have to let me down at the last minute. At my age I have got used to that tone of despairing jocularity from my coevals – and indeed from myself.

I was exhausted because the flight had been late in starting and even later in arriving; because, despite a pill and three whiskies, I had slept little between neighbours who had snored grossly on either side of me; because, waiting on and on for a guide who never arrived in the now deserted airport, I had staggered into the hotel more than an hour after midnight.

I was depressed because the overhead light in the bedroom was so dim and the bedside light did not work; because, as I shuffled in stockinged feet into the bathroom, cockroaches scuttled away from me; because there were beige stains caked on the bath and brown stains caked on the lavatory bowl and one of the two skimpy towels had all too clearly been used.

Then it was that I surprised myself. Each morning an old man puts on his Burberry and his hat, takes his stick, and lets himself out of his front door. He must be careful of that cracked paving-stone just beside the gate, since once he caught the toe of his shoe against it and had a nasty fall (all falls are now nasty). He turns left, as he always turns left, and he crosses the road by the lamp-post, as he always crosses it. He looks at the display in the window of the antique shop, although it rarely changes, and he peers through the glass door of the restaurant beyond it to see if that skittishly attractive Polish waiter has arrived for work, although he rarely has. Now he turns left again, as he always turns left. That is his walk each day. That is his day, week, month, year.

But that evening the old man failed to do the expected. He did not, with an effortful gasp, haul the suitcase up on to the bed and begin to unpack it. He did not place the shirts one on top of the other in the drawer, which mysteriously smelled of rotting apples. He did not hang up his two tropical suits from wire coat-hangers in a cupboard which tottered towards him as he pulled at its creaking door. He did not brush his teeth with mineral water from the otherwise empty mini-bar (the toothpaste making the water fizz frenetically in his mouth), carefully comb his grey, thinning hair and swallow two Temazepam tablets in a doomed attempt to fend off jet-lag. All

[8]

these things he did much later. For once, at long last, the old man surprised himself. As he emerged from his house, he had, in effect, forgotten his Burberry, his hat and his stick; and, when he reached the gate, for once, after so many days, weeks, months, years, he instantly turned not left but right.

The youth lolling in the chair by the door stared at me with the same intensity with which he had stared at me when, a suitcase in one hand and a brief-case in the other, I had first entered. The taxi-driver, having heaved my luggage out of the boot of his Lada, had not offered to help me to carry it in; and the youth, whom I had supposed to be an employee of the hotel, had not offered to help me to carry it in either. Later, I was to learn that employees of the hotel who wore such elegant shoes, such beautifully pressed trousers and such expertly laundered shirts were not there to offer help to the guests. They were there for a totally different purpose.

Out on the pavement the air was still hot. It was also heavy with a smell of fermentation, similar to that smell of rotten apples which, the next day, was to seep out of the drawer in which I eventually laid out my shirts. A single tourist taxi was stationed at the rank. Approaching it, I realised that it was the taxi which had brought me to the hotel. The obese, jolly driver, had chatted away to me in Spanish even though, knowing almost nothing of the language, I was incapable of answering him; now, his round, balding head lolling back and his mouth sagging open, he was clearly asleep. In the excitement induced by my late arrival in this hot, dark, mysterious city, I had perversely thought him sexy, even fantasising about those far from clean hands, thick hair on their backs, moving over my body or my own hands moving over

[9]

his. Now the driver looked totally unsexy. He might have been a corpse.

There was virtually no traffic in the road, the aorta of the city, which separated the hotel from what I realised was a small public park. I was soon to discover that at all times there was virtually no traffic, other than bicycles. These bicycles were usually all devoid of bells; so that as they winged in silently from behind one, one would all at once be startled by a whistle or yell of warning. Two women sauntered past me, swinging wide hips encased in glittering silver lycra. They peered at me, bending their heads forward and sideways, as though I were much shorter than they. Then one said to me in English 'Excuse me – are you Canadian?' When I shook my head, the other said 'You want good time?'

Of course I wanted a good time. Who doesn't want a good time? But I didn't want a good time with either of them. Even a good time with the taxi-driver would have been preferable. Again I shook my head.

Hands on hips, heads now thrown back, they stared challengingly at me. Then one of them emitted a derisive laugh. She turned to the other and hissed something in Spanish. Now the two of them laughed together. *Silly old queen!* It was unlikely that either was saying anything of that kind. More likely it was *He's past it! Why on earth are we wasting our time?* But people like myself are given to paranoia, and so it was something like that that I imagined.

I was amazed by how many people, some seated alone or in couples on benches, some sauntering arm in arm or hand in hand, some clotted in groups under trees, were still in the park. It was now almost two o'clock. I felt tipsy, in part at least from fatigue but in part, I convinced myself, from that strange fermentation of the air. I

[10]

staggered as I stepped off the road on to the crumbling pavement and then staggered again as I stepped off the pavement down on to an expanse of parched grass.

As I wandered down one alley of trees and then another, I kept thinking: How beautiful they are! Yes, men and women, they were beautiful, despite the conditions of near-starvation in which, for months now, they had been struggling to live. I stared, head turned, at one particularly beautiful young man, with thick, curly black hair and a shirt open to the navel, who was lolling on a bench, both arms outstretched along its back-rest as though in crucifixion. *What the fuck are you staring at?* Or: *Do you want something?* That, as likely as not, was what a young man like that would have snarled at me in England. Not here. The young man smiled. An invitation? Or merely a friendly acknowledgement of the presence of an obvious foreigner? I walked on.

Two youths, one muscular and black and one slender and white, approached me.

'Hello there!'

'Hello.'

Was I about to be mugged?

They edged in close on either side of me, so that I could smell the peppery odour, not at all disagreeable, of their sweat. Did I want to buy cigars? Did I want to change money? Did I want a girl, a beautiful girl? To each question I shook my head.

They did not persist. 'Okay! Okay!' The muscular, dark youth raised his hands, palms towards me, as though in acknowledgement of a truce. Then they sauntered on, the muscular and dark one having thrown an arm round the shoulders of the slender and white one.

Although it was so hot, suddenly a shiver slithered through my body. *A goose must be walking over my grave.* I

[11]

could hear my mother, long dead, say it. From time to time I have this eerie sensation that, from another room or from some place just out of sight above me, she is speaking to me. We were always close. There are times when we are close even now.

Where had the couple come from? They were nowhere and then they were there. They looked as if they had suddenly alighted, two exotic birds, from the roof-terrace of the hotel, where (I was later to discover) there was each night some performance of some kind – 'folkloric dancing' as a poster in the foyer advertised it, or salsa music, or jazz – and where, into the early hours, the tourists danced on and on above a city turning restlessly over and over in a sleep troubled by fitful nightmares.

I thought at first that the man, with his narrow face, hooded eyes and hair that seemed to have been carved, in deep, backward-flowing waves, from obsidian, was wearing a dinner-jacket. But the bow-tie was not black but red, and the suit was in fact made of a shiny dark green material which I took to be silk. The woman was in a wispy, diaphanous black dress, cut low in front, and in extremely high-heeled court shoes with diamanté buckles which glittered in the light as she extended first one foot and then the other, as though in a vain search for a comfortable way of standing.

What were they saying to me? And what was their nationality? With their air of wealth and elegance, it seemed impossible that they could be Cuban. Later, I was to decide that they must have been Colombian.

The man was speaking English, with a trace of an accent and, yes, with a slight lisp, as though each word were a pip that kept getting stuck to his teeth or his lips as he tried to spit it out.

Now the woman was speaking, with a sudden

urgency. She might have been telling me something of vital importance to me, to herself and her companion, or perhaps to all three of us.

The man and woman were offering me something. At long last I grasped what it was. *Coke.* That was the word I kept hearing. *Coke. Cocaine.*

The man put a hand, long and narrow like his face and with yellow, highly polished nails, on to the sleeve of my crumpled linen jacket. He squeezed my arm. 'Yes?'

*Surprise me!*

'Yes. All right.'

I went with them, in silence, across the park and under some trees – I could hear a girl giggling and could just make out two shapes, the giggling girl and the man astride her – and then on to the cracked pavement on the other side. There was an ancient American car, an Oldsmobile, parked by the kerb, its original yellow paint patched here and there with other, darker shades of yellow, so that its skin looked like that of a bruised pear. There was a diagonal crack across its windscreen, and one of its front lights had been smashed in some long-ago collision, so that all that was now left of it was an eyeless socket streaked with rust like dried blood.

The man opened the rear nearside door of the car and signalled to me to enter. I did so, collapsing on to the cracked leather seat. The woman got in on the other side, beside me. The man clambered in in front.

The woman was asking for money. Twenty dollars. Could it really be as little as that? I had no idea.

*Surprise me!*

I jerked my wallet out of the breast pocket of my jacket and took out first one ten-dollar bill and then another. I handed it to the woman.

The man in front was at his preparations. He leaned

[13]

over, careful not to spill any of the precious dust from the card extended to the woman. She slithered along the seat towards me. She held out the slim, metallic funnel. Momentarily I wondered: Is it made of silver? She nudged me – as though to say, take it, take it! I took it. I bent my head forward. I snorted and snorted again.

I waited.

Nothing happened.

Now the man was snorting. Now she. She threw back her head and began to laugh. Then the man too was laughing.

Still I waited.

Nothing had happened.

I thought: Nothing is going to happen. But if what they had given to me had been something other than what they had promised, why were their bodies still racked with convulsions of what must surely be cocaine-induced mirth?

I tumbled out of the car, all but falling to the ground. As I staggered away, I could still hear their laughter.


The young man in the chair at the entrance to the hotel was almost asleep. He stirred at the sound of my entering and looked up at me, no longer with the veiled hostility of before but with a kind of dreamy, bewildered welcome.

'Goodnight,' he muttered. With the tips of the fingers of his right hand he slowly caressed his right cheek.

'Goodnight.'

Still I felt nothing.

There was a cockroach, black and shiny as jet, on the edge of the wash-basin. I marvelled that, as I approached, it did not scuttle off. What courage to confront me like that, daring me to squash it! Then, as I gazed down at it, I realised that it was dead. How had it died, there on the edge of the wash-basin, suddenly, to all appearances in the prime of life while busying itself with some errand?

I flicked it away with the handle of my toothbrush, so that, legs in air, it now lay on the floor, and then held the handle under the trickle of water which was all that emerged from the hot-water tap.

How had it died? The question baffled and disturbed me.

# 2

Three hours later I awoke. It was not the usual slow, infinitely laborious surfacing up and up and up through sludge, to arrive, exhausted by the effort, eyes blinking and mouth agape, into consciousness in a cocoon of bedclothes. I was asleep, I was awake. It had happened as though at the click of a camera shutter. I jumped off the bed, hurried over to the windows and tugged back first one unlined curtain and then the other to confront the pearly dawn. I gazed out, across the aorta of the road, on to the park. Even at this hour there were people in it.

How strange. There was no sense of constriction in my chest, I felt no need to cough and hawk and spit. My bladder did not seem about to burst. My mouth was not parched. My head, so far from resembling some sealed, over-crowded storeroom, was now a vast, open arena, full of light and air. *I haven't felt like this for years.* What had happened to me? I was no longer sixty-nine. I was now sixty, now fifty-five, now fifty, the spool of time racing backwards. I was full of energy. After the depression of the previous evening, I was full of an unaccountable joy.

As I approached the wash-basin, I saw the corpse of

the cockroach, legs in air, on the tiled floor beside it. Without any of my former revulsion, I picked it up, so stiff and dry that it might have been a shard of ebony, and dropped it into the lavatory bowl. I flushed. Water trickled down. I flushed again. Now in a swirl of water, the cockroach rotated as though it were alive and frenetically swimming. When the swirl had subsided, the cockroach was still there.

Suddenly, as I gazed down at it, I felt as though something were also rotating within me, faster and faster. A machine, long since unused, had come to life at a touch on the switch. Scattering dust, it began slowly to turn over. Then it accelerated, gathering ferocious momentum.

While I waited for the beige-stained bath to fill from taps that now dribbled and now spat, I saw again the narrow, silver funnel and the valley of the card – a large visiting-card? – in which the precious ash had nestled. But I still failed to make the connection.

That only happened when, washed and shaved, I lifted my brown linen jacket off the back of the chair where I had hung it and was about to slip my right arm into its sleeve. On the sleeve there was a faint dusting of ash. I raised the sleeve to my nostrils and sniffed and sniffed again. Then the unexpected explosion of a sneeze convulsed my body.

That machine within me whirred faster and faster, giving me an extraordinary sense that its movement was displacing the random accumulations of years. As in some washing-machine, illusions and disillusions, apprehensions and misapprehensions, defeats and disappointments and doubts swirled round and round until they all seemed to merge into an iridescent foam.

*It must be a delayed action.*

But was that possible?

[17]

# 3

That morning, oblivious of the people outside the hotel who had eaten no breakfast at all, I ate a breakfast such as I had not eaten for years. There were cold, clotted scrambled eggs, pawpaw and mango fresh from the refrigerator and bejewelled with moisture, chill, glistening slices of ham, liver sausage and salami, muesli, brioches, croissants, cardboard-like slices of toast, coffee thick with grounds, tea the colour of straw. In one corner of the restaurant sat a group of black people, sombre and solemn, wearing tee-shirts with things like LOVING GOD IS LOVING OTHERS and MY BEST FRIEND IS JESUS inscribed on them. One of them, sniffing at the coffee-cup which he had just filled at the buffet, complained to me in a Caribbean accent: 'This milk must be off.' He held the cup out. 'What do you think?' 'It doesn't smell too good,' I said. The man had a little goatee and there were chunky rings on all his fingers and even on one thumb.

There was now another young man on duty by the door to the street, but standing, propped against the wall, not sitting. He scrutinised me coolly and carefully and made no response to my nod and smile. He too wore elegant shoes, beautifully pressed trousers and an expertly laundered shirt. Around his attractively thick neck dangled a plaited gold chain.

I crossed the park, still buoyed up by an energy such as I had not enjoyed for years. Under some trees, an untidy group of men appeared to be engaged in some kind of political altercation, to the blare of an ancient radio placed on a concrete bench beside them. Politics – *here?* Was it possible? I loitered on the ragged fringe of the group. One man, stout and sweaty-faced even at that comparatively early hour, was particularly vociferous, throwing up his arms as though in protest or stabbing with the forefinger of one hand, in a fierce eagerness to make his views known. A skinny youth turned to me and explained: 'Baseball.' All that vehemence was about nothing more serious.

Now I was walking up what once must have been an elegant street towards the Plaza de Armas. Dangling from one of my hands was a Harrods carrier bag containing a guidebook, a packet of cigarettes and a pullover which I certainly would not need. I peered through the door of now one dilapidated palace and now another to observe how the once soaring rooms had been divided horizontally to make two or even three storeys. Seeing me, a toothless old woman, perched on a chair in an entrance, in what appeared to be a nightshift, beckoned and croaked 'Come, come, come!' I smiled and shook my head.

Touts constantly approached me. 'You Canadian?' 'No.' 'Where you from?' 'England.' 'You want cigars? Very good cigars. Cheap, cheap, cheap.' 'No.' 'Why you no want cigars?' It would have been so much easier to ignore them. But I suffered from my upbringing. To ignore people, even strangers, when they ask a question is rude: sixty, sixty-five years ago my mother first told me that. I could not forget it, not even in this alien place.

I was looking up at the crumbling fabric of a church – there was a jagged wound at the top of its tower, as though a shell had ripped through it – when I heard a patter of feet behind me. Then, all at once, the carrier bag was no longer in my grasp. A black boy of ten or eleven, his bare legs like sticks and his bare torso emaciated, was racing off ahead of me, his head lowered in the manner of a rugby football player determined to touch down with the ball.

It was years since I had run, really run. But now I ran. I even ran fast. As I ran, I shouted, absurdly, in English: 'Stop thief! Stop! Stop!' Then everyone in the street was running with me, some ahead of me, some behind me, some at my side. The street reverberated to the clatter of innumerable feet and the shouts of innumerable voices. I ran effortlessly, with no breathlessness whatever.

The boy, head still lowered and the carrier bag clutched to his skinny chest with one hand, swerved down a side-street. Like a flock of birds, everyone gyrated. Then, far off, I saw a police-car approaching. The boy tried to dash into a house but a woman lolling on its crumbling steps barred his way with an out-thrust arm. He looked over his shoulder, he looked to right and left, he even looked (so at least it seemed) in imploring panic at me. The police-car stopped. Two uniformed men got out of it. With the flat of his hand one of the men hit the boy across the head, almost knocking him to the ground. The other man grabbed him by an arm, which he twisted behind his back. The boy let out an eerie scream. The noise was hardly human; it sounded like that of some small, vicious animal as the teeth of a trap snapped on its leg.

[20]

Handcuffed, the boy was flung into the back of the car. Everyone in the crowd was now shouting either at the two policemen or at the boy. My carrier bag lay in the road. I approached it. But before I could pick it up, an elderly man in a neat but threadbare suit, with a gaudy tie and a battered panama hat, had stooped and retrieved it for me. 'Look,' he said. He opened it. 'Everything here? Look.'

I peered inside it. 'Yes,' I said. 'Everything seems to be there. There was nothing of importance in it,' I added.

The old man smiled, revealing ill-fitting false teeth. Then he put a hand to my shoulder and patted it, not once but repeatedly as though he were patting a dog.

One of the two policemen now touched my arm. He indicated the car. I was to get in beside the boy. Reluctantly I did so. The policeman clambered in beside me. The car was so small that I could feel one bare arm of the boy pressing against mine, and one knee of the policeman hard against my thigh.

'Where are we going?'

The policeman merely smiled, teeth white and large under a luxuriant black moustache. Clearly he knew no English.

Suddenly I was aware that the boy's body, so close to my own, was being convulsed by shiver after shiver. For me, in that cramped car, it was intolerably hot. But the boy was shivering. Then I was aware of a smell, ammoniac, disagreeable. It emanated from the boy. It was the smell of terror.

I turned my head and looked at him. But, eyes wide, he would not look back, continuing to stare out at the window beside him, while the crowds stared in, their faces ugly with anger.

At last the car moved off.

'Where are we going?'

Again I received no answer to the question other than a grin.

When our party arrived at the police station, two policemen rushed up to the car on the side where the boy was sitting. One pulled open the door and dragged him out by an arm. Meekly, head bowed as it had been bowed when he had raced ahead of me through the streets, he stumbled into the station between the two men.

I never saw him again. Or at least I do not think that I did. I will explain later why I can never be sure.

Benches were ranged round a bare, whitewashed room. A young woman, with glistening black hair and a glistening black face, sat behind a desk on a dais. She smiled at me in welcome, pointed at an empty bench and said 'Please.' The palm of the hand upraised to me was pink. She was beautiful, as so many of them were beautiful. I was not long alone on my bench. More and more people entered, spoke to the woman on the dais, were told to sit and wait. Eventually, when there was no room on any other bench, a tall girl, her lips a moist scarlet and her long lashes caked with mascara, seated herself nervously on the far end of mine. I took her to be a prostitute.

A young man, in jeans and a tee-shirt gaudily covered in a froth of white, red and pink roses, eventually swayed into the room. His hair stuck up in spikes; dark glasses covered his eyes. He pulled off the dark glasses with a histrionic gesture and looked about him. Then he approached my bench. As he seated himself, between the woman and me, he gave me a smile at once secret and intimate, a smile of complicity. The smile said: *Hello. I know what you are. You're what I am. But in this country neither of us must admit it.* I did not want to look at him again. His knowingness – *it takes one to know one* – had filled me with an irrational unease.

Minutes passed. People came in, people went out. Or, summoned by a shouted name or a beckoning finger, they made their way, sometimes hurrying but more often with a studied leisureliness, through a swing door into the interior of the building. Eventually, the young man, who had been sitting with one leg crossed high over the other, a cigarette held between the middle finger and the fourth finger of his left hand, rose at a summons. He pulled a little face, glanced at me, glanced at me again, this time with that same secret and intimate smile, that smile of complicity, and then, his body swaying as the bodies of the two tarts had swayed the previous evening when they had approached me, he walked towards the swing door. At the door he turned. Again that smile. I looked away.

The woman on the dais was glancing over at me. When our gazes met, she gave a little smirk, held out the watch on her wrist and then shrugged, as though to say: 'I'm sorry you're having to wait. I don't know why they're keeping you so long.'

A man with grey ringlets reaching to his shoulders, a withered arm, and skin puckered about his mouth and nose as though from some terrible burn, had been staring at me for a long time through the grubby plate-glass window on to the street. Now he limped in. He approached me, holding out the hand of the arm that was not withered, with an expression of intense supplication. Then he put the hand to his mouth, in a gesture of eating. As, inexplicably embarrassed, I pulled some peso notes out of my pocket, the woman on the dais shouted something. The man snatched at the notes and

[23]

whisked out. The woman seemed to be about to pursue him as she jumped down from the dais. Then, with a shrug and a smile at me, she gave up.

'Please, sir. I am ready for you now.'

The officer stood with the swing door resting against one of his massive shoulders. There was a look of impatience on his face, as though it was I who had kept him waiting and not he me.

I scrambled to my feet.

The officer smiled.

'Please.' He gestured to me to pass ahead of him through the door.

As I did so, the officer suddenly released the door, so that it banged against my arm. I thought: *The trap closes.* I had no idea whether the officer had released the door on purpose or not. He made no apology.

The room was small and windowless. An ancient air-conditioning machine kept up a constant keening in one corner of it, but it seemed to have made no difference to the temperature. The officer lowered himself into the chair on one side of a desk across which files and papers were scattered in confusion. Uninvited, I took the chair opposite to him. He searched among the files, then came up with one. He opened it. He looked up and gave me a reassuring smile.

'I am sorry. Maybe you have many things to see, to do. I am wasting your time. But – ' he shrugged the massive shoulders – 'what am I to do?'

'And what am I to do?'

'You?'

He was bewildered by the question.

'What do you want of me?'

'Ah!' He gave a spontaneous, joyful laugh, such as I was often to hear him give in the days ahead. 'What do I

[24]

want of you? I want a statement. But first – I want your names.'

'Baker. Elliott Baker. Baker is my surname.' I pronounced the two names loudly and slowly.

The officer repeated them as, frowning, tongue sticking out between regular, white teeth, he began to write them down. 'Excuse me – how do you spell the first name?'

I told him. It took him a long time to get it right.

'And your work?'

'I no longer work. I'm retired.'

'And your work before you retired?'

'I was a civil servant.'

'Ah!' He grinned. 'Like me.'

I thought that there was little resemblance between working for the Treasury and working in a Havana police station. But I nodded and gave a small smile. 'Yes,' I said. 'Yes.' I almost added: 'I also write biographies.' But then I remembered that in countries like Cuba the authorities tend to be suspicious of writers.

The officer explained that the deposition must be in Spanish for the court. I should tell him what had happened in English and he would then translate it as he went along. I could then sign it – 'If you trust my translation,' he added, with that same spontaneous, joyful laugh. 'If you trust me.'

'Yes, I trust you.' I found myself laughing too. 'Of course I trust you.'

'Come and sit here. Beside me. It will be easier.'

When, dubiously, I rose to my feet, he at once leapt up and moved my chair for me. I sat down close beside him and, as I did so, I was suddenly aware of his smell. In that country where soap was now in such pitifully short supply, that smell suggested a fanatical cleanliness. The smell was strangely familiar to me, a smell from the far-distant past. At my public school the boys had been obliged to use Wright's coal-tar soap. Could it be that somehow he had come into possession of a cake of it – or of something similar?

As, our heads lowered, our bodies almost touching, we struggled to write the deposition, I all at once felt that machine once again whirring away, faster and faster, within me. My temples began to throb with its shaking, my mouth to feel parched.

At last, in his small, neat handwriting, as of some painstaking schoolboy at work on a prize essay, he had finished. He pushed the paper towards me. 'Please sign.'

I signed.

He stared at the signature, then burst into laughter. 'Who can read this?'

'My bank manager once told me that the less legible a signature, the less likely it is to be forged by anyone else.'

He looked puzzled. Probably he had not understood.

'Now you are going back to your hotel?' he asked as he held open the swing door for me to pass through. In the deposition I had had to give the name of the hotel, eliciting from him an impressed 'Very expensive' – although in fact, by English standards, it was cheap.

'No, not yet. I'll go on with my sightseeing. I was on my way to the Plaza de Armas when my bag was snatched.'

'Please be careful. People here are honest but some people are poor, very, very poor.'

*Some* people? Surely most people? But I did not say it.

'Have a good time. I was happy to meet you. I hope we meet again.'

[26]

'Yes, I hope so.'

I knew that all at once I was sounding awkward and formal. On such occasions I am like a tennis player who, faced with an important match, stiffens fatally with nerves.

# 4

I was sitting in the vast, almost deserted bar of the hotel, with a sandwich and a glass of vodka on the rocks on the table before me, when to my amazement I saw the officer approaching. Previously he had been wearing his uniform trousers and a shirt open at the neck. Now he was also wearing a black tie and his uniform jacket. In one hand he was holding a cap, its brim thick with plaited gold and silver braid. He looked elegant but for his shoes, which were scuffed and cracked across the insteps.

He smiled, extending both his hands in greeting. We might have been old friends who, after a long search, had at last encountered each other.

'I have found you!'

What did he want of me, I wondered, less than two hours since our previous meeting? My joy at seeing him was tempered by apprehension. I had already told him, in vain, that I did not want the boy to be prosecuted. Even more strongly I did not want to waste any further time.

'May I?' He pulled back the chair opposite to me.

'Please . . . What would you like to drink?'

'It is forbidden to drink on duty.'

'Some Coca-Cola? Surely that's allowed.'

It was easy to persuade him. Coca-Cola was obtainable only for dollars in tourist bars and hotels. He shrugged. 'If you wish.' He leaned forward and peered into my glass. 'What are you drinking?'

'Vodka.'

'You should drink Havana Club 7. That is what Ernest Hemingway drank. That is the best drink in Cuba. Rum.' He turned away, to beckon to the waiter. Then, although I had drunk only half of my vodka, he ordered me the rum.

No doubt muzzy with lack of food and the heat, the waiters were usually lethargic. But this one, having taken so long with the vodka, soon hurried over with the Coca-Cola and rum.

'Try,' my visitor urged me, pointing at the glass.

I sipped.

'Good?'

'Very good.' Indeed, it was good.

'Now you must always drink Havana Club 7.'

Having sipped and sipped again at his Coca-Cola, with obvious relish, he leaned forward across the table to explain the reason for his coming. I had praised the police for their efficiency in catching the boy, hadn't I? And I had praised all the people who had joined me in the chase?

I nodded.

Again he leaned across the table. Would I be prepared to write a letter to the Minister of the Interior putting this on record?

I was taken aback. Why on earth should he want this of me? I hesitated. Then I said: 'Well, yes. If that's what you would like.'

He went on to explain. The tourist trade was now

extremely important to Cuba. I knew that, didn't I? If that trade was to grow, it was essential that prospective visitors should realise that the country was safe for them. Of course from time to time, since some people were so poor, a theft – such as I myself had experienced – unfortunately took place. But thefts of that kind were far less common than in New York or even – he gave a rueful smile – in London. In Cuba no tourist ever got mugged, he had never heard of such a thing. But unfortunately guidebooks and foreign newspapers too often wrote about the dangers of Cuba. Such dangers hardly existed. If I were to take a walk late at night through the old city, I would be perfectly safe.

I did not tell him that the previous night I had taken such a walk. I nodded. Yes, all right, fine. I'd write the letter. Perhaps, I thought to myself, such a letter would gain him a commendation or even promotion. Perhaps that was the real reason for his asking me to write it. 'You'd better give me the name and address of the minister.'

He frowned, sipping at his Coca-Cola. Then yet again he leaned across the table, glass still in hand. I noticed how beautifully manicured his nails were, buffed to a shiny pink against the brown of the surrounding skin. 'I think it is better if you send the letter to your ambassador and ask him to send it on.'

'Oh . . . Why?'

He shrugged. 'I think it is better.'

'Oh, very well.' I was puzzled.

After some desultory questions – where did I live in England? why was I travelling alone? was I planning to visit any other places in Cuba? – he picked his cap off the table and got up.

'Many thanks. You have helped very much.'

[30]

On an impulse I said 'I don't know your name.'

He was taken aback. 'My name?' Then he gave that spontaneous, joyous laugh of his. 'My name is De León. Eneas.'

'Aeneas!' I pronounced it as the English pronounce it.

He smiled. 'Not a usual name. My father loves Greek and Latin literature.'

'Is he a professor?'

He shook his head. 'Doctor. Doctor of medicine.'

The young man stationed at the door straightened himself from his leaning position against the wall as we approached. Eneas gave him a curt nod, a superior to an inferior. Then he turned to me to ask: 'You wish to visit Ernest Hemingway's house?'

'Possibly.' I had no real wish to do so.

'I will take you. The Hemingway house is near my house, the house of my father. It is now a museum. In San Francisco de Paula. You wish me to take you?'

I was overjoyed by the thought of going anywhere with him. But I simulated casualness: 'Well, it's very kind of you. But aren't you far too busy?'

Tomorrow, he told me, was his free day. He would call for me at – would nine be too early?

I shook my head. No, nine would be fine, absolutely fine.

He held out his large, powerful hand. I shook it.

'You will not forget that letter?'

'No, I won't forget it.'

'And you will give it to your ambassador?'

'Don't worry.'


On my return to the bar, I ordered another Havana Club 7.

After the middle-aged waiter had set down the glass,

[31]

he hovered at the table. Then he said: 'The officer is a friend of yours?'

The same waiter had already asked me where I was from, what I did, what I was planning to do.

'No, not really a friend.'

The waiter smiled. His white monkey-jacket, though ragged at the sleeve-ends, was immaculately laundered. He had a large mole on one side of his beak of a nose. 'Today you have trouble,' he said.

I frowned in pretended incomprehension.

'That thief was black,' the waiter said, as though that were an explanation of the crime.

'He was probably hungry.'

'Many people in Cuba are hungry. They do not steal.'

When I had finished my drink and paid for it – it was difficult to attract the notice of the waiter, who seemed, like most Cuban waiters, to be determined not to produce a bill – I decided that, if I had to write that letter to the minister, I had better write it at once.

A pretty little maid was doing out my room. When I entered, she began hurriedly to gather up her bucket, brush and rags. I opened a drawer and took out a cake of soap. I held it out to her. For a moment she was reluctant to take it from me; then, suddenly, her hand shot out. She held the cake to her nostrils and sniffed at it, eyes half closed in ecstasy. When she opened her eyes, it was to repay me with a small curtsey and a smile. Then she slipped the soap into a pocket of her apron and scampered out of the room.

Composing the letter, I began to sweat, even though I had switched on the air-conditioner. It exasperated me to have to waste time on something so foolish. But if Eneas wanted this, then I must do it for him. I struggled to find the right sort of flowery phrases: I had been profoundly impressed by the efficiency and courtesy of the police, it had been heartening and touching to receive so much help and support from the general public, such an incident, though trivial, had shown the Cubans at their remarkable best. Well, if that didn't earn Eneas and his colleagues a commendation, nothing would!

I hesitated for a moment. Then I remembered that skinny, shivering body on the car seat beside me, and once again, as I drew a deep breath, I smelled that ammoniac, faintly disgusting odour. I added another paragraph: I could understand how, in the present economic situation, a young boy could be driven by hunger to such an action, I therefore hoped that the case against him could be dropped.

Having written a covering letter to the ambassador – what would he make of all this? – I set off for the embassy through sunbaked streets. Given the heat of the afternoon, they were now almost wholly empty of people or even of the stray dogs, many of them mangy, limping, emaciated, which had cowered away from me, growling and even baring their fangs, when that morning I had attempted to befriend them.

A sleepy girl with a Scottish accent – she yawned openly as I entered her cubby-hole of an office – took the letter from me.

'For the ambassador,' I said.

'I'm afraid H.E.'s on holiday.'

'Well, for the chargé d'affaires.'

She yawned again and turned away from me.

# 5

Again I woke early, just as dawn was breaking. I woke
with an extraordinary feeling of happiness, so that I at
once asked myself: *What is this? Why am I feeling like this?*
I had grown used to waking in my London house with a
headache, with an aching of the joints, with a feeling of
nausea, with a sense of foreboding, of guilt, of despair. I
thought of that ash-like powder. I thought of the extraordinarily beautiful young man – one of the most beautiful I had ever seen, I had by now convinced myself –
who, in a little more than three hours, would be calling
for me. Powder or young man, or both, could be the
cause of this otherwise unaccountable change in me, I
decided.

But suppose he did not come? Panic, like a sudden
upsurge of nausea, overcame me. But he would, he
would! I knew that he would.

It was years since I had moved so quickly and alertly
about the business of shaving and bathing and dressing.
I strode into the dining-room. Normally withdrawn, I
greeted the waiters. 'What a beautiful day!' I remarked
to one of them, and 'How are you today?' I asked of
another. I cried out to the members of the religious group

'Good morning! Good morning!'; and, surprised, they looked up and smiled and choirused something back.

Eneas was almost an hour late in arriving. I sat in the foyer, near to the door, so that I could see out through it to the street and, beyond the street, to the park. What had happened to him? Eventually I got up and, under the wary gaze of the young man on duty, peered out through the glass panels. The taxi-driver of my arrival was leaning against his taxi, while carrying on a conversation with a girl whom I recognised as the maid to whom I had given the soap. As the taxi-driver laughed at something he had said to her, he inserted a hand into his baggy trousers and unselfconsciously scratched at his crotch.

What had happened to Eneas? *What could have happened to him?*

At last I saw him through the glass door, hurrying across the park and then, dodging an oncoming bicycle, dashing across the street.

'Forgive me! Forgive me!' he cried out, his arms extended to me, as they had been when he had approached me the previous day in the bar.

'Don't worry! I knew that you would come.' But I had not known that, not after half an hour had passed. I had been racked with anxiety and dread.

Suddenly, to my amazement, he had thrown both his arms around me. He pulled my body close to his own, and then held me there for seconds on end. Involuntarily I stiffened, not yet realising that such a greeting between two men was perfectly normal in Cuba.

'Perhaps you understand that here we have a problem.'

'A problem?'

'When we wish to go from one place to another. Maybe I should have come on my bicycle. But it is very far.'

'Did you have to wait a long time for your bus?'

Eneas laughed at the naiveté of the question. 'Yes, yes. For an hour, more than an hour.' He must have noticed the look of incomprehension on my face. 'You do not realise the economic situation in Cuba?'

'I know that it's bad.'

'*Bad!*' Again he laughed. 'It is terrible. There is no gasoline and so there are no buses.'

'Then how are we to get to Hemingway's house?'

He shrugged. 'Taxi?' He pointed at the taxi which had brought me from the airport. 'But I am embarrassed. This is a dollar taxi. A taxi only for foreigners.'

'But you can travel in it?'

'Yes, I can travel in it. But I cannot pay for it.'

'Oh, don't worry about that! I'll pay for it. I have lots and lots of dollars.'

The thought of spending money on him filled me with excitement. Soon I was to understand how friends of mine had lavished money, often far more than they could afford, on buying watches, shirts, cuff-links, ties, suits, shoes for their boyfriends. Until I had met Eneas, I myself had never done anything of that kind.

The taxi-driver recognised me. First he pointed at me with a forefinger, grinning his pleasure. Then 'Okay? Okay?' he asked me, pumping my hand. After that, he and Eneas entered into a conversation during which I heard the name 'Hemingway' repeatedly. Then Eneas pulled open the door and nodded at me to get into the taxi. He clambered in beside me.

Unselfconsciously he sat right up against me, leaving a space between himself and the further side of the Lada. His bare arm was across the back of the seat, behind me; I could feel his fingers resting lightly on my shoulder.

[36]

But although all this would have meant something in England, perhaps even a lot, I knew that here it meant nothing at all. When I had signed the bill for my breakfast that morning, hadn't the waiter put a hand on my shoulder, as he had leaned over me? When I had tipped the taxi-driver, clearly far too generously, after that drive in from the airport, hadn't he thrown an arm round me and briefly hugged me to him?

Eneas began to explain the difficulty of getting a taxi in Havana if one was a Cuban. But he did so as though it were all a joke, with no bitterness or resentment. Such taxis as there were, were almost exclusively for the tourists, he said. The month before, his grandmother, his father's mother, had collapsed with what was later diagnosed as a near-fatal heart attack. No neighbour had the petrol – gasoline he called it – to drive her to the hospital; and frequent telephone calls failed to bring either an ambulance or a taxi. Fortunately his father had then returned home and treated her.

'Everything here seems to be in short supply. Except, of course, for us tourists.'

'Yes, everything. Everything!' Eneas gave that spontaneous, joyful laugh of his. I might have made some joke.

Soon, impelled by that curiosity which invariably overcomes me when with someone who attracts me, I began to ask him about his life. Without any hesitation, totally candid, he gave his answers. His father had wanted him to be a doctor like himself; but he had never studied hard enough at school and had therefore failed to get into university.

But he seemed so intelligent, I protested, his English was so good.

[37]

He squeezed my shoulder in pleasure. Was his English good? Did he really seem to be intelligent? The problem was that during those years he had wasted so much time.

'On what? On what did you waste it?'

'Girls.' He threw back his head and laughed. 'And body-building.'

'*Body-building!*'

'I wanted to have a beautiful body because I wanted to have beautiful girls.'

'Well, you got the beautiful body. Did the beautiful girls follow?'

He nodded seriously. 'Yes. Many.'

A vanity which certainly would have irritated and exasperated me in anyone else only endeared him the more to me.

'But now I have given up body-building. Six months ago I weighed two hundred pounds. Now I weigh one hundred and seventy. To practise body-building it is necessary to eat a lot. In Cuba no one now eats a lot.'

He went on to relate how, before he joined the police, he had worked as a stevedore. He had done it to improve his body. But the pay was bad, bad. In any case, with the economic crisis, there was less and less work in the docks. There would always be work for a policeman, he added; in Cuba policemen would always be needed. I could well believe that.

The gates to the Hemingway house were closed, even though my guidebook and the taxi-driver both said that they should be open. Eneas pushed at them and then, with the sudden rage of a thwarted child, kicked at them. The taxi-driver waddled off to a corrugated iron shack close to the gates. An elderly woman in gym-shoes appeared, shielding her eyes from the glare with a hand. By her side was a grey, shaggy mongrel which kept up a low growl; it was emaciated, its eyes rheumy. She and the taxi-driver talked together interminably. What could they have to say? I wondered. Then Eneas went over to join them.

Eventually Eneas returned to the taxi. 'Yes, it is closed,' he confirmed.

'But why? Why?'

He shrugged. 'She does not know.' He gave that laugh totally devoid of any bitterness. 'This is Cuba. Have you forgotten?'

I wanted to ask: 'What on earth have you been talking about for all this time?' But I merely said: 'Well, what shall we do instead?'

'The beach?'

'Yes, why not?' Normally, on holidays, I avoid beaches, with their dazzle, their heat, their monotony, their crowds. But I was already excited by the prospect of seeing the Cuban strip off his clothes – the blue jeans, the tee-shirt through which the swelling pectorals and pro-tuberant nipples were excitingly visible – and exhibit that body-builder's physique in all its grandeur and beauty.

'Maybe it will be too expensive to take the taxi to the beach.'

'Oh, to hell with the expense!'

While Eneas swam, in his underpants, far out to sea, I lay out under a twisted tree from which blossoms, smelling of cinnamon, trailed in luxuriant pink-and-white chains. I had never before seen one like it. The taxi-driver sat asleep at his wheel, mouth open. The exhilar-ation of my waking had not left me. I felt full of energy. I was ready for anything.

Suddenly I saw that Eneas, now in the shallows, was talking to a girl with large breasts and haunches and

[39]

long, dark hair. He raised an arm and splashed her with water. She let out a scream. He splashed her again. Then she splashed him. My happiness briefly curdled into an unreasoning jealousy, such as I had not known for many years.

Then he was racing up the sand towards me. Had I seen his butterfly stroke? That was his best stroke. He had swum for his school. He was the school champion in butterfly.

Yes, terrific, terrific, I said, although I was incapable of differentiating between butterfly and crawl.

Once again, there was something touching, even attractive about his vanity.

Now, standing before me, he began to strike poses and flex his muscles in the manner of a contestant in a body-building contest. When, at one moment, I was distracted by a group of middle-aged Canadians trailing wearily up the beach, their voices raised in some argument about a boat which they had or had not hired, he called for my attention: 'Look! Look!'

'Beautiful.' I meant it.

He grinned with pleasure, like a small boy showing off for an adult.

At last the exhibition had finished. He threw himself down on to the sand beside me.

'When there is more food in Cuba, I will start body-building again.' He sighed in sudden and uncharacteristic discouragement. 'When!'

On an irresistible impulse I asked: 'Who was that girl?'

'Which girl?'

'The one to whom you were talking just now.'

He shrugged his massive shoulders, grinned. 'How do I know? I talked to her. That was all. You liked her?'

Now I shrugged. 'She was all right. Too fat.'

[40]

'Cubans like large women. Big bosom, big – ' He rolled over and patted one of his buttocks.

The beach was now deserted. The tourists had returned to the hotels which; like so many concrete chests of drawers, were stacked untidily round the bay. The Cubans – I had no idea where they would have gone. Such hotels would not be open to them.

'Hungry?'

'Very hungry. Now at home we do not eat breakfast.'

'Why not?' In retrospect, I was to be ashamed of my obtuseness in putting the question.

'Because there is not enough food for three meals. We eat in the evening when my father returns from his hospital.'

'Shall we go and eat now?'

He lay back on the sand and closed his eyes. 'In a moment.'

Instantly he appeared to fall asleep. I watched him, at once detached and overwhelmed by his beauty. At that moment there was nothing sexual in the intensity of my admiration and love for his body.

Far off, I could see a small, solitary figure trailing laboriously across the burning sand. It was a girl, the wind blowing her long hair across her face and jerking at the skirt of her simple cotton dress, so that with one hand she kept attempting to keep it in place.

Suddenly she saw the two of us under the tree. She paused, a hand raised to shield her eyes. She changed course. She began to make her way towards us.

She must have seen Eneas when he was swimming or when he was posing, I decided.

I watched her as she trudged purposefully up the steep rake of the beach. Then I realised, with astonishment, that all the time she was looking not at Eneas but at me.

[41]

When she was about twenty yards away, she halted, breathless. She was still looking at me. 'Hello,' she said. She had the voice of a child.

She was pretty. She was also slim and frail, so that it was unlikely that she would instantly attract Eneas or any other Cuban man.

'Hello.' I smiled at her, even though I was irritated by her presence.

Eneas opened his eyes and sat up to look. Then he fell back on the sand. I had been right. She did not interest him.

Uninvited, she lowered herself on to the sand at my feet. She put up a hand and removed my dark glasses. She looked into my eyes. 'Beautiful eyes,' she said. 'Blue eyes.'

I laughed, as I reached out and took the glasses from her. Then I replaced them on my nose.

Again she put out her small hand, the nails savagely bitten. She touched my Marks & Spencer shirt. 'Beautiful shirt.'

'Thank you. I've never thought much of it myself. I don't know why I bought it.'

'You Canadian?'

I shook my head. 'English.'

'Ah, English! I like English.'

'Have you met many English?'

She did not answer. She pointed at Eneas. 'Your friend?'

'Yes.'

'Cuban friend?'

'Yes.'

'You like Cuba?'

'Of course.'

There was a silence, during which she stared appraisingly at me.

Then she said: 'Give me cigarette.'

[42]

When she had drawn one from the packet which I held out to her, she stared down at it. Then she said, pronouncing the words with difficulty: 'Benson and – 'edges.'

'That's right.'

'I like Marlboro.' She had no problem in pronouncing that word.

'I'm afraid I don't have any Marlboro.'

With difficulty, shielding my lighter from the wind, I lit her cigarette for her. She sucked on it greedily once and then again. She put her head on one side. 'Good,' she said.

I began to ask her about herself; and, rummaging in her memory for words, she managed to answer me. She lived in Havana, with her parents, a brother and two sisters and her two-year-old son. She was a widow. Last year her husband, a truck-driver, had been killed in an accident. Life was difficult, no work, no food. Suddenly she looked as though she were about to burst into tears. She turned her head away from me, biting on her lower lip. Then, almost angrily, she said: 'Give me cigarette!' She had only just thrown away the dog-end, smoked almost to its filter-tip, of the one I had already given her.

As I again struggled with the lighter in the wind, she said: 'You lucky.' She said it with an intensity of bitterness.

'Yes, you're right. I am lucky.'

It is something I have often thought: how lucky I am to have been born into an upper-middle-class family, in a country of western Europe. I am one of a small and extremely lucky minority. Unfortunately members of that minority so seldom think themselves lucky; and when I tell them of their luck, they become resentful, irritated, exasperated, even angry.

'I wish to go to England. Or Canada. Or maybe

[43]

Mexico.' She looked up at me, with a cajoling expression, scratching at the same time at a bare calf with the thumb of the hand holding the cigarette. 'You help me?'

'I wish I could.'

Had Eneas made the same request to me, I should have answered: 'Of course! Of course!'

'Give me cigarette!'

'Do you think you ought to chain-smoke?'

'Chain-smoke?'

'Smoke one cigarette and then another and then another.'

She shrugged. 'If one smoke, one does not so much want to eat.'

The word 'eat' acted as a reminder. I looked at my watch. Then I looked across at Eneas. He appeared to be asleep.

'Eneas!'

He stirred and gave a little whimper, but did not open his eyes. The girl laughed. Then she put out a foot and, to my amazement, dealt him not a prod but a real kick. He sat up. He glared at her. Then, when she again laughed, he joined in her laughter.

'Oughtn't we to go and get some lunch? It's past two o'clock.'

He reached out for his tee-shirt and began to struggle into it. As he raised first one arm and then the other, I saw the dark, moist hair in each armpit.

'You go eat?' the girl enquired.

'Yes. It's getting late.'

She again tilted her head to one side, with the cajoling smile. Then she said: 'I come too?'

I pretended either not to have heard her or not to understand. As Eneas got to his feet and began to pull on his jeans, I was watching the shadow of his cock and

[44]

balls through the damp fabric of the underpants in which he had been swimming.

'I come to eat with you?' she insisted.

I hesitated. Then I said: 'I'm sorry. I've already invited my Cuban friend and the driver of our taxi. One more . . .' I shrugged.

'You do not wish me to come?' Suddenly she was truculent. Her once-pretty face looked ugly as she squinted up at me, she still seated, arms around slim legs, on the sand, and I now standing above her.

'It's not a question of wishing . . . It's a question of money.'

'But you have money, plenty money!'

'Not all that much.'

I stooped and picked up the Harrods bag – the one which, the day before, the skinny black boy had attempted to snatch. I had remembered that in it I had some boiled sweets bought that morning from the dollar shop in the hotel. I took out the packet. 'Would you like these for your son?'

She stared up at me, still hostile. Then, without a word, she put up a hand and took the packet from me. 'Okay,' she said, as though she were consenting to do me a favour.

As Eneas and I walked off, she remained beneath the tree. She was smoking yet another cigarette, once again begged off me, her arms still around her knees and her head on one side as though listening for something. As I looked round to see her for the last time, I felt a terrible guilt and also the sort of anger provoked in one by the person, however innocent, who is the cause of one's guilt.

'I suppose she's a prostitute,' I said, as though that would somehow make the guilt less.

Eneas had thrown an arm around my shoulder, pro-

[45]

pelling me forward, as we trudged, behind the puffing taxi-driver, who had now joined us, up to the hotel. 'Prostitute! No, no. Not real prostitute. There are many such girls. What are they to do? No money, no work, no food. She comes here. Maybe she finds a Canadian, maybe she finds an Englishman – like you. Maybe she makes love. Maybe she is given a present.'

His words made me feel even more guilty.

The dining-room of the hotel was deserted but for two middle-aged Canadian women in bathing-costumes, who talked loudly at its far end. When the three of us had sat down, Eneas indicated this couple with a nod of the head and then pulled a face. 'Ugly,' he said. 'Why are foreign women so ugly?'

'I don't find them ugly.'

'You are used to such women.'

I knew that Eneas would be hungry, and found an exhilarating pleasure in urging him to order more and more food from the English-speaking waitress who at long last, having put down the book she was reading, consented to attend to us. The taxi-driver, still unable to grasp that I spoke hardly any Spanish and so repeatedly addressing remarks in it to me, ordered whatever Eneas did: *moros y cristianos*, the traditional dish of rice and black beans; gristly pork steaks with peppers and yams; bread, slice after slice of bread; jam omelettes. I myself wanted nothing but a salad. I felt no hunger, I was full of energy. Some thirty years before, when I had been seriously overweight, a gay doctor friend in Brighton – later to die from a drugs overdose, whether accidental or deliberate was never established – prescribed for me amphetamine tablets. Then I had felt exactly as I felt now: without appetite, my body an empty, clean cylinder, through which energy pulsed irresistibly, tirelessly.

I was soon disgusted by the way in which the taxi-driver would stuff food into his mouth, gulp down beer on top of the food, and then, with no attempt at concealment, belch and belch again. But Eneas ate with the same ferocious, crude zest as the driver and he disgusted me not at all.

'Why do you eat so little?'

'Because, unlike you, I had a large breakfast.' Suddenly I thought again of the girl abandoned on the beach. 'I wish I'd asked that girl to eat with us.'

Eneas pulled the same face as he had pulled at the Canadian women. He shook his head. 'Ugly,' he said, as he had said of them.

'Not at all. She was rather sweet.'

'Ah!' He burst into laughter, although his mouth was full. Then he playfully punched me on the shoulder. 'You liked her, you liked her!' He turned to the taxi-driver and said something to him in Spanish. The taxi-driver's small eyes almost closed as he concentrated on what he was being told. Then he, too, burst into laughter. He said something in reply.

'He agrees with me – she is too skinny.'

'It doesn't matter whether she's skinny or not, or ugly or not.' Suddenly I was angry. 'I ought to have let her lunch with us.'

Eneas stared at me for a moment. Then he popped a piece of meat into his mouth. He chewed. 'You cannot feed every hungry Cuban. There are many Cubans, there are many hungry Cubans.' He pushed his plate away from him and put out a hand. 'Give me a cigarette.'

The demand was as imperative as the girl's.

On the homeward drive along the highway between the long string of beaches and Havana, our car passed innumerable hitch-hikers. From each bus stop queues trailed away, some people standing, some squatting, some even lying where there was a grass bank or a verge on which to do so. I thought: How hot they must be, out there for minutes or even hours in the sun. Then I told myself: But they're used to this heat. That assuaged my guilt a little.

It might have assuaged it even more if we had picked up one or even a couple of the hitch-hikers. But I was in no mood for us to do so. As our car had bumped along, the driver had repeatedly slowed its pace whenever we were about to pass a group of girls. Then he and Eneas would both lean out and emit piercing wolf-whistles or shouts in competition with each other.

'I do wish you wouldn't do that,' I said at last.

Eneas grinned, not taking me seriously. 'But the girls are so beautiful!'

'It's so childish. And vulgar. Educated people don't do that in England.' Suddenly I realised how insular and prissy I sounded. I felt ashamed.

Eneas looked mortified. He shrugged. Then he leaned forward and said something to the driver. The driver turned round. He looked at me enquiringly. Then he also shrugged.

'Oh, do what you like! Don't pay any attention to me. Go on! Don't worry!'

But the wolf-whistling and the shouting stopped.


That evening Eneas and I ate at a restaurant described in my guidebook as 'Hemingway's favourite watering-hole'. To me that was no recommendation; but Eneas said that it was somewhere where he had always wished to go and so, inevitably, I took him there.

The décor, with its pink flock wallpaper, pink table-linen and chandeliers far too large and far too many for the room, suggested the restaurant of a two-star hotel in Brighton or Blackpool. When I put out a hand to touch the flowers, I found that they were plastic. Apart from a large, noisy party of Latin Americans – they were from Venezuela, Eneas announced after chatting to a girl of the party on his way back from the lavatory – the place was empty. A waiter in what appeared to be loose-fitting purple pyjama-trousers and a purple shirt, worn outside the trousers and held in at the waist with a yellow sash, started telling Eneas what was on the menu. Clearly he was recommending something.

'Do you think you could tell him that I'd like to *see* the menu?' I eventually interrupted.

Eneas passed on the request and sulkily the waiter went off.

'He has told me what is best. I do not need to see the menu.'

'Well, he hasn't told me, and I do.'

When the menu arrived, I began to scan it. There were separate sections in Spanish, English, French, German.

'What has he recommended to you?'

Eneas told me. It was the dish which appeared in the English menu as 'Various Grill' and was described as consisting of beef fillet, pork chop, chicken supreme, kidney, liver and fried egg. The cost was forty-two dollars. I almost said: 'You can't possibly have anything so expensive.' But then I decided 'Oh, give him what he wants!', as I was so often to decide in the future.

Eneas worked away doggedly at his huge and luxurious plate. But suddenly he had become quiet, even morose. What had gone wrong? I had no idea. Was he tired, ill at ease in a place so 'smart', feeling unwell, bored or fed up with talking English? I could only guess.

Then, in a challenging voice, he asked: 'Why did you come to Cuba?'

'Oh, for a variety of reasons. For the climate, to escape the English winter. And to see this beautiful baroque architecture before it all disappears.'

'Disappears? Why should it disappear?'

I shifted in my seat. 'Well ... eventually ... Won't things change here? The system will change and the Americans will arrive. And then the old houses will be pulled down to make way for hotels and casinos and department stores.'

Eneas went on eating.

'Yes?'

'You think the system will change?' Now the tone was not merely challenging, it was aggressive.

'Yes. Don't you?' Head lowered over his plate, he did not answer. 'Don't you want it to change?'

'What does it matter what I want?'

I decided to say nothing more.

We passed the rest of the meal almost totally in silence.


Out in the park between the restaurant and the hotel, I said: 'When shall I see you again?'

'Do you wish to see me again?'

'Of course!' How could he ask the question?

'Tomorrow I must work. But perhaps tomorrow evening ... I wish to take you to listen to some salsa music. You like salsa?'

'I've never heard it.'

'Do you want to hear it?'

'Why not?'

[50]

We arranged at what time Eneas would come to fetch me from the hotel. Then, as we were about to say goodbye, he said: 'I think that I take some leave.'

'Some leave?'

'Now I can have leave. Maybe I take it. Then I can be with you. If you wish me to be with you.'

'Of course I wish you to be with me.'

'Are you sure?'

'Of course I'm sure!'

# 6

The next morning I again awoke with a feeling of extraordinary happiness, and again I felt totally well. That day I would see Eneas. Admittedly it would not be until the evening, but I would see him.

To pass the time until our meeting, I decided to get in touch with a gay man to whom a gay Dutch friend, a diplomat once *en poste* in Havana, had given me an introduction. The gay man, who was named Raul, was not on the telephone. I looked up where he lived on my map and decided to call on him, unannounced.

It took me some time to locate the small archway, let into a high wall, with the number 13, scarcely visible, scratched into its masonry. There was a courtyard, in which an old man, with a long white beard flowing out over his chest, sprawled out on a wicker couch, asleep or in a semblance of sleep. Could this be Raul? I stood over him for a moment, uncertain whether to wake him or not. Then a young woman looked out of a window and said something in a high, scolding tone of voice.

I said Raul's name and, when she looked nonplussed, repeated it.

She pointed to a door in one corner of the courtyard.

I knocked. Inside I heard the yapping of what must, I decided, be at least three dogs. No one came. Again I knocked.

I could hear bolts being drawn. Then the door creaked open a chink and an unshaven face, the pointed chin dark blue, appeared around it.

'Raul Cutino?'

Glittering eyes squinted at me. 'What do you want?' a phlegmy voice demanded.

'I'm looking for Mr Cutino, Mr Raul Cutino.' I was wishing that I had never come on the errand.

'Come back in twenty minutes. You have woken me.' It was then past eleven.

'Oh, I'm sorry.'

'In twenty minutes.'

'All right.'

Suddenly a tiny Pomeranian, a wide, pink ribbon tied round its neck, rushed out from round the door and began to yap at my heels.

'Tina! Tina!'

Tina paid no attention, now not merely yapping at my heels but giving my ankles little nips, until I had reached the door from the courtyard out into the street.

When I returned, Raul was dressed in a towelling dressing-gown, open to reveal blue jeans and a tee-shirt. He was still unshaven; his long, narrow, bare feet, the nails curving round the toes, looked grey and grubby. He was fifty-three according to my Dutch friend, but looked at least ten years older.

'Who are you?'

Behind a barricade of wooden chairs, piled on top of each other to block off the room in which we were standing from the kitchen beyond it, three Pomeranians,

[53]

all, like Tina, with wide, pink ribbons tied round their necks, kept up a ferocious barking.

Against this cacophony I began to repeat that I had an introduction to him from our mutual friend.

At once he cut me off: 'I mean, what is your name?'

'Elliott. Elliott Baker.'

'Baker? Baker? I have never heard such a name.'

'Well, that's what it is. It's very common in England.' I laughed. 'I'm sorry. I can't do anything about it.'

In a deep, slurred voice he began to sing: 'Baker, baker, bake me a cake . . .' Then he broke off and pointed ahead of him. 'Please – Mr, er, Baker man.'

The room, all its windows shuttered and sealed, was uncomfortably hot. This, I thought, was what a prison-cell must smell like, when, all cramped together, a dozen or so men had slept in it for days and days on end. I guessed that the dogs must often piss and defecate indoors. There was a large, low central table, on which were piled books and newspapers. Glasses also stood on it, often with a rusty sediment in them, and ash-trays overflowing with cigarette ends. Books soared in precarious cairns, waiting to be demolished by a single misjudged footstep.

Raul shouted at the three dogs, without managing to silence them, and then began to cough. It was a bronchial cough, like my own, now miraculously cured, as early each morning I creaked down the staircase of my London house to get my breakfast. He drew a crushed packet of cigarettes out of the pocket of the dressing-gown, after a lot of fumbling and cursing under his breath, and placed one in his mouth. He sat down on the only chair not covered in books and papers, raised one skinny leg high over the other, and reached out for some matches.

I looked around me and, uninvited, eventually

[54]

removed the debris covering a chair and gingerly lowered myself into it.

Raul put out a hand for a half-empty bottle of rum in the middle of the table. He tipped some into one of the soiled glasses and gulped. He did not offer me any.

I held out the carrier bag which I had brought with me. Our mutual friend, I explained, had sent some presents.

With a grunt, he took the bag and rummaged inside it. His hand eventually emerged clutching a bar of soap. I had never before known soap to have so much importance in the lives of people. He examined the bar, then held it up to his nostrils, sniffed and sniffed again. It had come from a well-known supermarket. He pulled a face.

'Is this good soap?'

'Yes. I think so. I've never used it.'

'Then you are a wise man!' He gave a catarrhal chuckle. 'It smells *terrible*.' He leaned across the table, thrusting it out. 'Smell.'

I smelled. Then I shrugged and turned my head away.

'I am surprised that Rudolf should send me such a soap. He is a rich man, isn't he?'

Again I shrugged.

One by one, he took out the other things in the carrier bag. Some Floris Elite Cologne pleased him rather more, as did a tee-shirt with a map of the London Underground system on it.

'Did Rudolf give you any dollars for me?' he squinted up to ask when everything that the bag had contained was scattered around him.

'Dollars? No, I'm afraid not.'

'How strange! Very strange!' Again he squinted across at me.

[55]

I wondered, uncomfortably, whether he suspected me of having stolen the dollars.

Now he began to ask me about Rudolf. Was he enjoying life in England? Had he found himself a boyfriend? Did he plan to revisit Havana?

Then he began to ask me about myself. Why had I come to Havana? Had I come by myself? Why wasn't I staying in the Hotel Nacional, that was the best hotel of all, couldn't I afford it?

Repeatedly the thin, hairy arm reached out for the rum bottle. I almost said 'Do you think I could have some of that too?' But somehow good manners restrained me.

After he had yet again gulped at his glass, he stared fixedly at me, with bloodshot eyes under shaggy grey eyebrows. 'You are homo,' he said at last. It was a statement, not a question.

I smiled. Then, after a moment, I said: 'Yes, that's right.'

'Cuba is not a good place for homos.' He raised a hand and wagged his forefinger. 'Be careful, my friend. Be very careful.'

'What could happen to me?'

'Many things, my friend, many things. At best – robbery, maybe, or some embarrassing hours in the police station and some even more embarrassing hours at your Embassy. At worst . . .' With his hand he made a gesture of cutting his throat. 'Last week the body of a Canadian was found on the beach. Dead. Like that.' He repeated the gesture. 'He had been cruising the Malecón – you know the Malecón, the sea-front? – late at night.'

'I don't think I'm likely to be rash.'

'Every homo says that.' With a grimace of contempt, he stubbed out his cigarette. Then he looked up: 'You know my story?'

[56]

I hesitated. Rudolf had told it to me. 'A little of it,' I said.

Wearily, as though under a compulsion yet again to tell something which he had told over and over again, he embarked on it. I knew, of course, he began, that he was descended from a famous Cuban family – a family famous both in the cultural and the political history of Cuba? I knew, too, that he was a painter, yes?

I nodded.

A painter who did not paint! He gave a self-lacerating laugh, then began to cough. His mouth filled with phlegm which, head uptilted, he proceeded to swallow with difficulty. He had been famous as a painter when a young man. But now . . . he was – smashed. *Smashed*. He repeated the word, an odd one. I knew about the condition of Oscar Wilde when he came out of Reading Gaol? Well, that was his own condition when he came out of the concentration camp. Smashed. Physically and psychologically and socially smashed.

Suddenly I noticed that there were tears in his eyes. Were they there from his coughing or the smoke wreathing up from the cigarette between his nicotine-orange fingers? Or were they there from rage or exasperation or self-pity?

It had been in the sixties, he explained. El Commandante – he rolled out Castro's title with satiric magniloquence – had pronounced that homosexuality was a bourgeois perversion. A bourgeois perversion! Could I imagine anything more absurd? Why he, Raul, had buggered a number of Castro's soldiers. He had even buggered one of his officers on that bed over there. He pointed at a grey tangle of sheets on a pallet in a corner of the room. But it wasn't for any of those adventures that the police had come and dragged him off. No, they

[57]

didn't arrest people for what they had done but merely for what they were. Like the Nazis with the Jews.

The squalor of his appearance and his house, the yapping of his wretched little beribboned dogs, his rudeness, his total self-absorption: all these had set me against him. But now, involuntarily, I found myself succumbing to compassion.

'That is my story,' he concluded. He held out both his hands, rings on almost every finger, as though he were making some presentation to me. 'Interesting, yes?' Again he gave the catarrhal laugh.

'We gays in England constantly complain. But in comparison . . . What have we got to complain about?'

He glared at me. 'Why do you use that horrible word?'

'What word?'

'*Gays!* I hate that word.'

'Well, it's better than queers.'

'No, no! It is not better, not at all. We *are* queer. That is what we are.'

Soon after that, I said that I ought to be going.

'Why? Why so soon?'

I might have replied, Because your house stinks, and you haven't offered me a drink, and I don't really like you. But I lied. 'I have an appointment with a friend. I'm meeting him for lunch.'

'What friend? Who is this friend?'

'You wouldn't know him. He works at our Embassy.'

He grunted in obvious disbelief.

At the door, he said: 'You want some sex, safe sex?' As I hesitated for an answer, he went on: 'I will arrange it for you.'

'No, no. It's not necessary.'

'I will arrange it.'

I guessed that he had arranged sex for Rudolf. What

other bond could there have been between two men so totally unlike each other?

As he shook my hand – his palm was hot and clammy, as though he were suffering from a fever – he repeated: 'Your name is very strange.'

'It's very common in England,' I told him again.

'I find it very strange.'

'Well, as I said before, I'm sorry but there's nothing I can do about it.'

Once again he began to sing: 'Baker, baker, bake me a cake . . .' Then he gave a sudden, brief, braying laugh. At the sound, the three dogs again began to yap.

# 7

This time too, Eneas was late. But now that I knew that to be late was something usually unavoidable in Cuba, I did not worry about it. Once again I seated myself in one of the wicker chairs in the foyer, in a position where I could look out through the door into the street and on to the park beyond it.

A mini-van drew up and, clutching wilting bunches of flowers, the passengers stepped out of it. That morning they had appeared for breakfast soon after I had done so, their English voices gratingly loud and their laughter gratingly obtrusive as they had asked each other how they had slept and had joked about the inadequacies of the plumbing and the lack of anything but bottles of mineral water in their mini-bars. Like the religious black group, now apparently gone, many of them wore tee-shirts declaring their faith: but instead of slogans about the love of God and the redemptive powers of Jesus, these displayed icons of such people as Ho Chi Minh, Che Guevara, Mao Tse Tung and El Commandante himself. Later I had seen them clamber into the mini-van, no doubt on their way to some model nursery or clinic or factory.

Now one of them, a middle-aged, red-faced man with a Yorkshire accent, in an aertex shirt and linen slacks supported by a belt under a swelling beer belly, did not join the rest to pick up his key, but instead came over to me.

'Excuse me. You are English, aren't you?'

'Yes.' I tried to sound as unwelcoming as possible.

'You didn't happen to see a young girl, a Cuban girl, looking rather lost, did you?'

'No. I don't think so.'

'We had a date – have a date.' He gave me a conspiratorial grin. 'We met out there' – he indicated the park – 'last night when I was taking a little stroll before turning in. I said I'd meet her at six, but we were held up at this school, the pupils insisted on putting on a concert for us, and I'm afraid she may have been and gone.'

'Transport is so bad that Cubans are almost always late.'

Without asking, he lowered himself with a grunt and a sigh into the seat opposite to me and took a pipe out of the breast pocket of his shirt.

After a lot of striking of matches and puffing at the pipe, he at last managed to get it lit to his satisfaction. He sucked contentedly. Then he sighed again:

'Beautiful country!'

'Yes. Very beautiful.'

'Have you ever seen such beautiful women?'

'Yes, they are beautiful.' I was tempted to add: 'And the men are beautiful too.'

'In Santiago I met this real stunner. Well, first I met her sister, she was not bad, but this one . . . You've never seen such boobs!'

He went on to talk about all the women whom he had bedded in the course of his tour.

[61]

Then, in a tone which differed not at all – it pulsed with the same kind of barely suppressed sexual excitement – he spoke of Castro. What a marvellous man! What charisma! And, though he was now in his sixties, he was still so handsome, so youthful, so energetic! They had had the privilege, he and his crowd, the extraordinary privilege – it was something they had never expected, not in a hundred years – of an audience with him. Of course it was only a minute or two. It was amazing that such a busy man could spare even that for them. But he had, he had!

He held out his pudgy right hand, a heavy gold bracelet dangling from its wrist. 'Yes, that hand has shaken the hand of El Commandante. Now that's something to tell my grandchildren when I get home.'

I wondered how impressed his grandchildren would be.

Suddenly he jumped up. 'There she is! She's out there!' He pointed through the door. Then he rushed out.

Seconds later, he was ushering the woman into the hotel. She was unusually tall, her hair piled in serpentine coils on top of her head to make her look even taller. There was a look of unease in her eyes. As he walked past me, he lowered a hand on to her bottom and patted it twice with perfunctory briskness. Then he looked over his shoulder and gave me a wink.

Soon after that, Eneas arrived.

He greeted me with none of his usual exuberance, mumbling: 'Sorry, again I am late, sorry,' as I grasped his unresponsive right hand in mine.

'What's the matter?'

'What do you mean?'

'You seem worried – depressed. Not your usual self.'

He sank into the chair in which the Englishman had

been sitting. He leaned forward in it, hands crossed before him and head lowered, so that I could not see his face.

'What is the matter? What is always the matter? Why should I tell you and spoil our evening together?'

'Because we're friends.'

He turned his head sideways and gave a little laugh.

'Aren't we friends?'

Now he looked at me. 'If you say so.'

'Of course I say so.'

He gazed around him, with a kind of puzzled, uneasy wonder. The English party had reappeared, washed and changed. The Yorkshireman who had talked to me was not among them. 'Where's Tel?' I heard one of the women ask, and a bearded young man replied with a laugh: 'Oh, he's got other things to occupy him.' 'Really!' the woman exclaimed, in disapproval. 'That man has only one thing on his mind.'

Eneas said: 'Sorry. My mood is bad.'

'Well, that's perfectly understandable. If I were a Cuban, my mood would be constantly bad.'

He looked at his watch. 'I have had another idea for this evening. I will take you to see other dancing, folk-dancing. You have heard of the Katumba Company?'

I shook my head.

'It is the best dance company in Cuba. It has visited Mexico, Russia, Bulgaria – oh, many places. Maybe England.'

'All right.'

I was unenthusiastic; and I must have sounded unenthusiastic because he now said: 'If you do not wish to go, you need not go.'

'No, I'd like to go.'

The theatre was little more than an extremely long,

narrow room, in effect a tunnel, with chairs ranged in unraked rows at one end of it and its other end masked by a shiny green curtain, sagging in irregular folds from a buckling rail.

As we entered, Eneas told me in a low, hissing voice: 'You must pay in dollars. I am sorry. Tourist means dollars. Always, always.' It was the first time that I had encountered him in this mood of sustained bitterness. It was not to be the last.

In return for the dollars, we were marched up to the front row of the chairs by the female usher. Brusquely she dislodged a woman with a child on her lap and the man with her, and then indicated to us that we should sit in their places.

'Oh, I don't want to take their seats,' I protested. 'I don't mind sitting at the back.'

'Sit. You have paid dollars. Sit,' Eneas repeated, pointing at the chair.

If he were in that kind of mood, then it seemed to me both unwise and useless to oppose him. I sat.

On and on we waited. People came in, people left. Groups encroached on the stage to carry on animated conversations with each other. The child whom the usher had displaced produced a ball with which he began to play with another child. At one moment the ball bounced off a wall and hit me on the shoulder. Eneas shouted at the child, as he angrily picked up the ball and lobbed it back. Everyone else was laughing at the mishap.

Some men who were clearly the musicians walked in and then, a few minutes later, walked out again. A dancer emerged from the wings and did some practice handstands on the stage before sauntering off it to talk to a woman in the audience.

'What are we waiting for?'

[64]

Moodily, Eneas shrugged. 'You wish to go?'

I did wish to go. But I said: 'No, of course not.'

The performance, when at last it started, was one of astonishing energy. Probably these dancers were as ill-fed as their compatriots. But one would never have guessed it as they bounced, pranced, leapt and raced about the stage. From time to time Eneas would try to explain to me what was happening – that character over there was a barren woman eager to conceive, that one in a mask was a demon, that was the god of war. But I took little in. The din and frenetic movement had had a literally stunning effect on me.

In the protracted interval – there was no bar and, when I suggested that we might go out and find one, Eneas said fretfully: 'Where? Where? Are you crazy?' – a tall, thin, handsome man, with the proudly strutting walk of a dancer, came over and greeted Eneas. He was a member of the company, Eneas explained when he introduced him, not dancing that night because of an injury to his knee. The two Cubans began a conversation in Spanish, during which they edged closer and closer to each other and spoke more and more quietly, with more and more smiles and giggles. At one moment, the dancer put up a hand and stroked Eneas's cheek with the back of it. It was what an adult might do affectionately to a child. It seemed an odd thing to happen between two men in public. I felt a sudden, rasping suspicion. I had convinced myself, though there was so little evidence of it, that the dancer must be gay.

With a hug, the dancer eventually took his leave of Eneas. As he walked away, he turned his head and called out '*Adiós!*' to me. He raised a hand and wiggled its fingers in farewell. Yes, he must be gay, he must be!

'Are you old friends?'

[65]

Eneas shrugged. 'We were at school together. We do not have many things in common, not then, not now. But he is a good boy. Very successful.'

Eventually, after more than half an hour, the performance was resumed. By now I had wearied of the pounding music, the frenzied dancing. It was all too monotonous for me. Dare I suggest to Eneas that we should go? Frowning in concentration, he seemed to be wholly absorbed. But of course it was possible that he was absorbed not in the show but in his own problems.

I had been astonished by the overt sexuality of many of the movements. One could not imagine such frankness being permitted in a similar dance performance in the former Soviet Union or any of its satellites. Often the women's breasts were bare, and repeatedly the men touched them and even caressed them. On three separate occasions a male dancer mounted a female one in a simulation of intercourse, with a lot of ludicrous writhing, gasping, moaning and contortions of the features.

Suddenly, at what I assumed must be the climax of the show, since every performer was now crowding the stage, the most attractive of the female dancers detached herself from the rest and shimmied over to me. She stood in front of me, gyrating her hips, while her red skirt swayed from side to side. I surprised myself by feeling a sexual excitement. Her legs were long, brown, beautifully shaped; her bare breasts were perfect, their brown nipples surrounded by large, purple areolae. Everyone in the audience was now looking not at the stage but at me. I could hear laughter. Was it derisive laughter at the spectacle of an old man being made to look a fool by a young woman? I could not be sure.

Then, with a leap, she was astride me, her arms around my neck, her breasts pressing against me. I could smell

[66]

the potent odour of her body. It reminded me of the smell of guavas. She was glistening with sweat. Throwing back her head, her mouth now stretched in a rictus which revealed regular, large white teeth, she began to mime the sexual act, jerking herself up and down on me. At first, as the laughter around me rose in a crescendo, I felt disgusted and angry. Then, all at once, I realised that I was getting an erection.

No doubt she felt the erection beneath her. Soon after, she disengaged herself and, having given me a roguish smile and a playful slap on the cheek, rejoined the rest of the company on the stage.

In the foyer, Eneas said: 'That was a beautiful girl. I think that you enjoyed her.' He put an arm around my shoulders and squeezed me to him. 'Yes? You enjoyed her?'

I laughed. 'It was all rather embarrassing.'

'But you enjoyed her. I know, I know!'

Could he have noticed the erection? It was years, thirty or forty years, since a woman had given me one.

'Would you like to meet her?' he pursued.

'Meet her?'

'It is easy. She is a friend of my friend – that dancer who talked to me. We can go behind and find her. You can invite her to dinner at the hotel. With me or without me,' he added. 'As you wish.'

'Don't be silly.'

'I am serious.'

'Don't be silly.'

# 8

Eneas had succeeded in getting his leave; but he would have to wait another day for it.

'I am sorry. What am I to do? Someone is sick, I must wait till he comes back.'

'I'll have to manage as best I can without you.'

At breakfast the next morning I sat glumly over a third cup of coffee, wondering how I should set about passing the day until Eneas arrived. I could go to the Columbus Cemetery or the Museo Nacional de Bellas Artes or to the Museo Nacional de la Música – where, my guidebook informed me, there was 'an extensive collection of bongos'. But somehow none of these prospects appealed to me. Perhaps I should merely continue with my rereading of *Les Caves du Vatican* in the foyer of the hotel or in the park opposite.

'May I join you?'

It was Tel, the Yorkshireman.

Without waiting for an answer, he lowered himself into the chair opposite, with a grunt followed by a sigh. 'My crowd left early this morning. They've gone to the Plaza de la Revolución. I overslept – not surprisingly after all my exertions!'

'What's there to see there?'

'Where?'

'At the Plaza de la Revolución.'

His mouth gaped open in a prodigious yawn, which he made no attempt to cover. 'Sorry. You can see the state I'm in. What's at the Plaza? Well, there's a memorial to this José Martí chap – you know who I mean, the father of independent Cuba, isn't that what they call him? I think we're supposed to be laying a wreath. And there are various ministries. And the Postal Museum – I'm sorry to miss the visit to the Postal Museum, I have quite a good collection of stamps myself – including one 5p Falklands stamp commemorating the marriage of Princess Anne to the Phillips twit. I bet you didn't even know that such a stamp existed.'

I sipped at my coffee, while he started on his cold scrambled egg.

Then he looked up and said: 'Well, what did you think of yesterday evening's date? Terrific to look at, wasn't she?'

Sipping again at my coffee, I made no reply.

He swallowed some more cold scrambled egg. 'And she was even more terrific in bed, I can tell you! The best I've had during the whole of this visit. In fact, the best I've had for *years* – though I wouldn't want the wife to hear me say that.' He laughed delightedly, throwing back his head. Then he leaned forward across the table. 'And do you know – all she wanted in the way of payment was a Max Factor lipstick and three cakes of soap. Just three. I couldn't believe it. I told her I'd give her the lipstick this evening. I imagine I can buy one at the dollar shop here in the hotel. I brought some soap with me, so that was all right. Our tour organiser told us to bring soap. It was like gold here, he told us. And he

[69]

was bloody right!' Again he threw back his head and gave the same delighted laugh.

'Well, I must be getting on with things.' I picked up my key and pushed back my chair.

'What are you planning for today?'

'Oh, I don't know yet.'

I feared that, if I were specific, he might offer to accompany me.

After a morning of lonely sightseeing and a lonely luncheon at the hotel, I lay out on my bed with my book, with the air-conditioner crooning away ineffectually beside me. Time was passing so slowly, and that fretted me with impatience. But at the same time I felt happy. That evening I would once more be with Eneas.

Suddenly the telephone on the bedside table began to chirrup.

'Yes?'

A voice, speaking in an all but unintelligible accent, told me that there was someone downstairs who wished to see me.

'Who is it?' But the phone clicked and went dead.

I jumped off the bed. I pulled on my shirt and trousers, slipped my feet into a pair of moccasins, and hurriedly ran a comb through my sparse hair. It must be Eneas. Who else could it be? Probably he had been allowed off earlier than expected.

There was a maddening wait for the lift; and then a no less maddening descent, as maids, their work for the day concluded, crowded in at each floor. They eyed me surreptitiously and then whispered, heads close, with occasional explosions of giggling. No doubt all foreigners seemed comic to them.

I stepped out of the lift and scanned the foyer. There

was no sign of Eneas, there was no sign of anyone I knew. Then a well-dressed man in a suit approached me.

Having established that I was the person for whom he was looking, he put out a hand for me to shake. 'Raul sent me,' he said.

'Raul?'

He nodded. 'Yes.' He smiled flirtatiously. 'He thinks we can be friends.'

I was nonplussed. But perfectly in command of the situation, he went on: 'My name is Cesaro. Forgive my English. I have not spoken English for some time. I used to speak English with Rudolf.'

'You know Rudolf?'

'Of course!' He gave a clear, rippling laugh.

Why 'Of course'? I wondered.

He took my arm, as though we were old friends. 'Do you know the terrace of this hotel?'

'No, I've not been up there.'

'Let us go to the terrace. Very beautiful view. And we can have coffee or a drink. Cuban coffee is not now so good, but there is rum, Cuban rum. Very good! Or European drinks, if you prefer them.' As he spoke, his hand now firmly gripping my elbow, he was propelling me towards the lift.

In the lift we looked at each other, he smiling, I sombre. He was older than I had first thought. His hair, so black and so shiny, must, I now decided, have been dyed. There were small lines around his mouth and at the corners of his eyes. Thirty, thirty-five, even forty? But there was no doubt that, with his straight nose, his thick, arched eyebrows and his strong chin, he was strikingly good-looking.

Like the restaurant when I had taken my lunch there,

[71]

the terrace was deserted. It was also hot, even under an umbrella. A waiter, even more lethargic than the waiters downstairs, eventually shuffled over to take our orders – an orange juice for me, a Scotch and soda for Cesaro – and, after many minutes, then brought them across.

'I have not drunk whisky for a long, long time. Not since Rudolf was here.'

'Yes, Rudolf always loves his whisky.'

I wondered how much the Scotch would cost. I also wondered why Rudolf had not told me of this friend of his.

'Do you like Raul?'

I was taken aback by the abruptness of the question.

'I hardly know him. He seems a – rather sad figure.'

'Sad?'

'Yes, sad.'

Cesaro pondered for a moment, glass in hand, as though I had said something difficult to follow. Then he said cautiously: 'Perhaps you are right,' raised his glass to his lips and gave a toss of his head and a shrug.

Soon after that he began to ask me about myself: How old was I, where did I live in England, how had Rudolf and I met, did I have a wife and children, what had I been doing since my arrival in Havana? He asked all these things with simulated eagerness; but he paid little attention to the answers, his eyes gliding away from my face, to look out over the balustrade of the terrace or across to the waiter.

Now it was my turn to put the questions.

'What work do you do?'

'Nothing!' He laughed. 'I have surprised you, yes? Once I worked in this hotel and once I worked in the international exchange of the telephone office and once I was a guide for Havanatours. But now – nothing! In

Cuba many people do nothing. Maybe next month I start work again in the telephone company. They always need speakers of foreign languages. *Maybe.* In Cuba nothing is certain.'

Next, I asked him whether he was married. He shook his head. Not now.

He had married when he was only seventeen, he had had two children. Then – he raised both hands and let them fall – divorce. No, he never saw his former wife, he never saw his children. He was here, they were at the other end of the island, in a village near Santiago.

I began to wonder: Why had Raul sent this man to me? What did he want? If he wanted what I thought that he wanted, then I did not want it at all.

'We go downstairs?'

I felt a grateful relief: by some miracle, he must have intuited my lack of interest in him. I got up from the table and pulled out my wallet. He looked over to the waiter and clicked the fingers of a hand. The gold Rolex watch which he wore on the wrist – could Rudolf have given it to him? – caught the late afternoon sunlight slanting across the terrace. The waiter showed no hurry. Cesaro still sitting, his arms resting on the table, and I standing, one of my hands resting on the back of my chair, we waited.

'Sit.' Cesaro smiled up at me as he said it.

I remained as I was.

The sum was far higher than I had feared. Should I leave a tip? As I hesitated, Cesaro said: 'Give him a dollar. A dollar is enough. In Cuba a dollar is a lot of money.'

I felt like saying: Even in England seventeen dollars is a lot of money for a Scotch and soda.

After we had got into the lift, Cesaro pressed not

ground floor but five. I decided that he must have seen the number of my room from the cumbersome key which I had placed on the table between us. We stood in silence as the antiquated lift creaked into action. We were very close, my back against one side of the lift while he, facing me, was all but touching me. He gave me a slow, conspiratorial smile.

When I stepped out of the lift, he stepped out with me.

I turned, about to say goodbye. But he put a hand to the small of my back and then propelled me, gently but irresistibly, down the corridor towards my room at the dark end of it.

'Look,' I began. Then I put the key in the lock and turned it.

He followed me into the room. What am I doing? I thought. But suddenly, surprisingly, I had felt a wave of excitement surging through me.

'You will give me a present?' he said, taking off his beautifully cut jacket – later I was to notice the Armani label – and carefully folding it before placing it over the back of a chair.

'What would you like?'

Remembering what Tel had told me about his girl's request for a Max Factor lipstick and three bars of soap, I expected Cesaro to ask for something similar. But instead, his head tilted to one side, he answered, in a tone of coaxing interrogation: 'Fifty dollars?'

'That seems an awful lot of money.' Had he not told me only a few minutes before that in Cuba one dollar was an awful lot of money?

'Then give me what you wish.' He shrugged. Now he was taking off his shirt. I could see that, though slender, his body was strongly muscled. The brown skin was smooth and shiny.

I put out a hand and stroked a shoulder. 'Glabrous,' I murmured. I have always liked that word.

'Please?'

'All right. Fifty dollars. But it does seem an awful lot of money.'

It was soon clear to me that what Cesaro was doing with me was done not from any inclination but for that awful lot of money. But, to his credit, he was determined to give value, and he knew how to do so.

The problem was that he could not achieve an orgasm. 'It doesn't matter,' I told him, 'forget it, it's not necessary.' By then, I myself had come and I was longing only to get rid of him, to have a shower, to stretch out on the bed with a mingling of self-disgust and weariness, and enter oblivion. But on and on he jerked, sitting astride me, mouth tensed into a line and eyes half closed with effort. I closed my own eyes. 'Forget it, forget it!' I repeated.

His breathing quickened, became a snorting. There was a groan, followed by another, even louder. Then suddenly I felt the warm, viscous fluid squirting over my left cheek and my chin. Cesaro was laughing. I too began to laugh, at the absurdity of it all.

'May I have a shower?'

'Of course.'

I lay on the bed, arms behind my head, listening to the noises from the next-door bathroom. He took a long time. When he emerged, he was smelling of my Caron Pour Un Homme.

'I like your perfume.'

'Yes. It's my favourite. I've used it for years and years. But the strange thing is – in this dry heat, it seems to smell far less strong.'

'May I take it?'

[75]

I laughed. 'No, I'm sorry. It's the only bottle I have with me. If I had another...' But even if I had had another, I doubted if I would have given it to him. He had begun to exasperate me and I wanted him only to go.

I scrambled off the bed and went over to my jacket. I took a fifty-dollar bill from my wallet and held it out.

He stared down at it. 'You have nothing smaller? In Cuba it is difficult to change so big a note.'

My exasperation intensified, I searched my wallet. 'I have only four ten-dollar bills here.'

No doubt fearful that I would give him the four ten-dollar bills instead of the fifty-dollar one, he said: 'Never mind. I will change it somewhere.' He plucked the fifty-dollar bill from between my fingers. Then he put up a hand and patted my cheek.

'Was that good?'

'Fine.'

'I am sorry that I was so long. But if one does not eat sufficient food . . .'

'Yes, of course, of course.' Suddenly, my exasperation gone, I felt sorry for him. 'It was fine.'

'We meet again?'

I shrugged. 'I have a lot to do, a lot of friends to see,' I lied.

'Let me give you my telephone number. If a woman answers, just say that you are telephoning about the Spanish lesson. You understand – the *Spanish lesson*. Tell her the convenient day and time but say the Spanish lesson. Then I will come for – ' he smiled, suddenly looking extraordinarily handsome – 'for your next lesson. Okay?'

'Okay.'

## 9

That evening I once more waited for Eneas in the foyer of the hotel. By now, the well-dressed young security officer, seemingly relaxed but always wary, on guard at the door, was prepared to give me a smile on each occasion when our eyes met. He had established that I was a friend of a colleague. If I were meeting that colleague, then I must be all right.

Tel hurried into the hotel with another woman, wide-hipped, wide-mouthed, heavily made up. He looked harassed, as though he either knew already that he had made a mistake or had had too little time to accomplish what he was planning. He did not even glance at me, as he passed me and, approaching the desk, barked out his room-number for his key.

When Eneas finally appeared, he once again seemed tired and discouraged. He did not embrace me, as he usually did, or even shake my hand. 'Sorry. Again I am late.' His voice was low and hoarse.

'Is anything the matter?'

He shrugged and pulled a face. 'Not a good day.'

'Sit down and have a drink. Then you can tell me about it.'

Again he shrugged, before reluctantly lowering himself into the chair which I had indicated to him.

'What went wrong?'

I had been feeling an acute guilt over my behaviour with Cesaro; and now I crazily persuaded myself that it was because of that behaviour – of which, by some miracle of surveillance or intuition, he had learned – that he was in this sombre mood. Or could it be that he had become bored with me, that he regretted having taken a week of leave merely to be in my company, that he would much rather have spent this evening with one of his girls?

'What went wrong?' I repeated, since, sitting awkwardly in the wicker chair, his body twisted round and his knees drawn up as though in a deliberate effort to be as uncomfortable as possible, he had given me no answer.

'They are stupid,' he said and stared out ahead of him, his lips compressed. I presumed that he was talking of his colleagues. 'Sometimes they are also bad.' He turned to me with a tentative smile. 'Let us forget them.'

'All right. Let's forget them. What'll you have to drink?' I looked around for a waiter.

'No drink.' He leaned over and slapped a hand down on my knee, so hard that the sting of it remained for several seconds. The mood, whatever its cause, had clearly passed. 'This evening I wish you to meet my family. Yes?'

'Oh . . . Oh, all right.' I was dubious. So often meeting the family of someone whom I have loved has proved to be an irretrievable disaster. 'Do you really think they want to meet me?'

'Of course! What are you saying? They wish very much

to meet you. I have told them of my new English friend and they wish very, very much.'

As we passed through the door, he put out a hand and patted the youthful security man standing beside it on the shoulder. '*Adiós!*' Then he turned to me, putting the same hand on my shoulder, to give it a squeeze: 'I have a surprise for you.'

'A surprise?'

'In a moment I will show you.'

He began to cross the road. As I followed after him, I did not bother to look to either right or left, so that a cyclist, swooping towards me without lights, all but knocked me down. '*Tonto!*' the cyclist yelled over his shoulder.

'What did he shout at me?'

Eneas laughed. 'Nothing too bad. We have many worse things to shout.'

He led me down a side-street. Then he pointed: 'There!'

For a moment of bewilderment and alarm, I thought that the ancient, ramshackle American limousine parked askew at the pavement was the same limousine in which, on the night of my arrival – how long ago it already seemed! – I had snorted that fine ash. But I had been mistaken in the dim light from a far-off street-lamp. This car was not the colour of a pear darkened here and there by bruises, but was painted silver, with blotches of grey and black where it had been marked by some collision. At the wheel, reading a newspaper held up to catch the frail light from that distant street-lamp, sat an old man, white-haired and with a face which would not have been out of place in Africa. His hands were long, the finger-joints knobbly. His wrinkled neck was encased in an extremely high collar, with a spotted bow-tie, red on navy blue.

The old man turned his head at the sound of our approach and then began carefully to fold up his newspaper. All his movements and his subsequent driving showed the same deliberation.

'Alonso, this is my English friend,' Eneas told him in English.

Alonso descended stiffly from the car. He held out his right hand. It felt dry, and strangely cold on that hot night, in mine. 'I have heard of you.' The accent was American.

'Alonso is our neighbour. You spend so much money, too much money, on a taxi. So I have an idea. For much less money Alonso will drive you.'

'Wonderful! What a wonderful idea!'

Eneas must have been doubtful as to how I would respond. Now he was not merely relieved, he was delighted. 'It is very old but beautiful, yes?'

'I have had this car for thirty-six years,' Alonso said. 'Thirty-six,' he repeated as though he could hardly believe it himself. 'Longer than I have had my wife.' He gave a hoarse laugh, the wattles of his chin shaking above the jaunty, made-up bow-tie.

Eneas and I clambered into the back of the car, which smelled of stale sweat, cigar smoke and leather polish. Unlike the other ancient car, this one had been lovingly maintained. Once again, as when we had travelled in the taxi, Eneas sat as close as possible to me, his body touching mine at hips, arms, knees.

'This is better than a taxi.'

'Much better.'

From time to time turning round, so that I wanted to shout at him 'Take care, take care! Something's coming!', Alonso began to talk in his deep, slow voice. He had

[80]

worked for an American company in the days of Batista. When the revolution happened he had been a fool. The American company would have employed him in Florida, they had offered to do so, but he had believed, idiot that he was, that Cuba would become a paradise. Well, he was young then, comparatively young, and the young always tended to believe that paradise was only a few metres away. Yes – he sighed – he had been a supporter of Castro. He had even provided the revolutionary government with information about the American firm, so that it had been easy to seize all its assets. But how had the glorious revolution ended? Well, I could see for myself.

I was surprised and uncomfortable that the old man should speak so freely in front of Eneas, a policeman.

Suddenly, at a traffic-light, the car stalled. Cursing under his breath, Alonso attempted to restart it, with no success. With a sigh, he opened the glove-compartment and took out a pair of white cotton gloves, which he pulled on. He clambered out of the car, other cars hooting as they swerved to avoid him, and limped stiffly to its front, where he jerked up the bonnet.

'Do you think we ought to try to help him?'

Eneas shook his head. 'He understands his car.'

'After so many years, he ought to, I suppose.'

As the two of us sat waiting in silence, I became increasingly aware of that body so close to my own. Then I was once again overwhelmed with shame and remorse for what had happened that afternoon. As though to assuage these feelings, I pressed my knee even closer to his. He made no withdrawal.

'What should I pay him?'

'Who?'

[81]

'Alonso.'

'What you wish. To take you to my house and back to the hotel – five dollars?'

'Oh, that seems far too little.'

'It is enough.'

That afternoon I had bought some presents for Eneas at the shop in the hotel. Now I decided that, in addition to the five dollars, I would give Alonso one of the cakes of soap and one of the packets of dried milk from the carrier bag on the floor beside me.

Alonso climbed back into the car and slowly peeled off first one of the gloves and then the other. Their white was now soiled. Twice the engine died on him; then it whinnied into throbbing life. He smiled over his shoulder. 'My car is like my wife. It sometimes takes a long time and a lot of trouble to get her to perform for me.'

Now he began to question me about Cuba. What did I think would happen? How long could Castro survive? Did I think that the American blockade would hasten his departure or only delay it?

I kept replying: 'I don't know. I just don't know.' Nor did I. I had read a few books about Cuba, I had talked to a few friends, like Rudolf, who knew the country. But really I was ignorant.

Suddenly Eneas joined in the conversation. Did I know that people constantly made attempts to sail or row themselves across the straits to Florida? Some neighbours of his had successfully done so. They had been a father and mother, two children, a grandmother, a dog. They had set off in a little fishing-boat. No one had thought that they could possibly make it. *Milagro!*

But not all people were so fortunate, Alonso took up. Eighteen months ago two students had secreted themselves in the undercarriage of a plane bound for Madrid. When the plane touched down, one of them was dead and the other had been totally deafened by the engines. He sometimes thought of trying to get out himself. But he was the sort of person who would be caught and either imprisoned or shot. He never had any luck.

By now we had turned off the main road to make our way down a side one, totally dark except for the wanly diffused light from the windows of the shack-like houses on either side of it. Then we turned down a road even more narrow. Through the window open beside me, stronger than the odours of stale sweat, cigar smoke and leather polish, I could smell what might have been the countryside instead of a suburb. I breathed in deeply. Bats were swooping low over the corrugated-iron roof of a little church. Alonso swerved to avoid a group of tiny children squatting in a ring, presumably at some game, in the middle of the uneven, dusty road.

'We have arrived!'

Eneas jumped out of the car, raced round to the other side of it, and jerked open the door. I emerged, the carrier bag in one hand.

He pointed. 'You can leave that in the car.'

'No, I can't. I have some things in it for you and your family.'

'No! *No!* Why do you do this?'

'Because I know of the situation here. And because I feel guilty at eating whatever I want whenever I want, while the Cubans are starving.'

Alonso had been listening. 'It is not for you to feel guilty. The guilt belongs to others.' His white jacket glimmering ahead of us, he began to mount the steps up to a house more substantial than any of the others in the dark, narrow street.

[83]

A dog began to bark. Then I saw it, thin and shaggy, with a huge, sweeping tail, in a wire enclosure in the garden. 'That is Dido,' Eneas told me.

Of course! What else?

'Take care!' Alonso warned, as I leaned over to pat the dog. But the warning was not necessary. I felt a long, gluey tongue gliding over my wrist and then my fingers.

The front door was open. An elderly woman stood in its frame, her head and shoulders illuminated by the light behind her. This was Eneas's grandmother, the mother of his father. She spoke no English at all; but, as in the case of the taxi-driver on the night of my arrival, this did not deter her from talking away at me.

She ushered me into a small, square sitting-room, its floor paved with marble chips and its walls white-washed. She pointed to an arm-chair and, as she did so, an old man, clearly suffering from Parkinson's disease, shuffled in in slippers. He took my right hand in his two trembling ones and said in English 'We are very happy, we are very honoured.'

I was left with him and Alonso, while Eneas and his grandmother went off to the kitchen to prepare some coffee.

The old man told me that he had been a school-teacher. He had taught English, he added with a wry smile, but now, after so many years of retirement, fifteen, sixteen years, he had forgotten so much. I must excuse his English.

'But you speak extremely well.'

'No, no! You are flattering me. You are flattering me.'

He and Alonso had been neighbours, he went on, schoolmates, friends at University. Together they had courted their wives, who were sisters.

'I am sorry that my son is not yet here. He works very

[84]

hard at his hospital and the hospital is so far away. He must bicycle there each morning, fifty minutes, and then he must bicycle back, fifty minutes again. But he will come, he will come! He too wants to meet you.'

The coffee arrived. Silent but pleased, Eneas sat in a chair behind his grandparents and Alonso, literally taking second place to them.

In turn the old people asked me questions. Then came the inevitable one: Was I married?

As in Italy, as in Greece, as in Spain, as in Japan – countries in which not to be married suggests some physical or psychological defect – I now lied. I was a widower, I said. My wife had died many years ago.

Had I any children?

I shook my head.

They all looked sorry for me.

Eneas jumped to his feet as though to unburden me of the embarrassment which I was all too clearly showing. Would I like to see the room which he used for his body-building?

I got up, relieved.

It was not so much a room as a cellar, with a low ceiling and a small, square window set high up in one of its raw concrete walls. A naked bulb dangled from a length of flex. In one corner there was a camp bed and, standing slightly askew beside it, a folding table, supporting what I later learned were the textbooks from which he studied English.

He went over to some rusty parallel bars and swung himself back and forth between them. Then, with remarkable grace, he did a somersault. He smiled at me, with that touching, inoffensive vanity of his, the vanity of a child. He continued to perform on the bars, while I, by now sitting on the sole chair, a hard, upright one,

[85]

watched him. I felt an extraordinary rapture, totally devoid of sexuality. It was a rapture similar to that which I had felt, an eighteen-year-old undergraduate on holiday in Florence in the immediate aftermath of the War, when I had for the first time looked up at Michelangelo's *David*. On that far-off occasion I had felt actually giddy with the rapture and had gone over to a wall and leaned against it, to steady myself. Now, too, I felt light-headed, as though, on a crazy impulse, I had gulped down a whole glass of spirits.

Eneas left the parallel bars and went over to the weights, also rusty, which were stacked in another corner. He pulled his tee-shirt up over his head, exposing his torso, and then, having removed the shirt, threw it across the room to the bed. He grinned at me. 'Hot.' He hefted the first weight with ease, emitting a groan, which was almost a yelp, as he did so. The next weight caused him more difficulty. Sweat ran down his chest between the swelling pectorals. His forehead was glistening with sweat and his whole face was unusually pallid. When he tried to lift the third weight, he struggled for a long time but each time failed. His frustrated efforts reminded me of Cesaro kneeling over me, his face contorted with effort and his breath coming in gasps.

Eventually, ashamed, he lowered the weight to the ground. 'No good.'

'But you did wonderfully with the others.'

'I have become weak. To be strong it is necessary to eat, eat, eat.' He lowered himself on to the bed. His head sank on to his chest. 'What is to happen to us?' he asked. 'We are all weak, weak, weak. Cuba is dying.'

At the time it seemed to me a melodramatic thing for him to say. But later, looking back, I have realised, with anguish for my obtuseness, that he was only stating the truth.

'Let us return. I think I heard my father.' He began to struggle back into his tee-shirt.

'You are very strong.'

'Once!'

'You have a beautiful body.'

'You think so?'

'Yes. Yes, I do.'

With quiet pleasure, he accepted my praise. It is impossible to imagine any heterosexual Englishman reacting in the same way – ' You must be joking!' or 'Oh, come off it!' or (hostile) 'Are you a poof or something?' would be the most likely response.

Eneas's father José was as handsome as his son and even taller. But cruelly thin, with hollow cheeks and bruise-like shadows under sombre eyes, he projected none of the same impression of physical strength and well-being.

'Forgive me,' he said, speaking with not so much a stammer as a brief hesitation before each of the words. Perhaps this hesitation was merely a result of his exhaustion. 'I was operating until late and then I had the long ride by bicycle home.' His English was far better than his son's, even better than Alonso's. I felt embarrassed that my presence in the house now prevented him from dining or resting. 'Please.' He pointed to the chair in which I had been sitting before. Recently re-upholstered and re-covered, it was clearly the best.

The same questions were asked, the same answers given. Then, in a curiously formal way, he said: 'I am grateful that you are interested in my son. He is a good boy but, as he may have told you, he was not a good student and wasted too much of his time. I think it will benefit him to talk English with you.' Could he have prepared this speech in advance?

'I'm very happy – and lucky – to have his company,' I replied awkwardly. Then I became aware that, seated in his old place behind his grandparents, Eneas was grinning down at the floor in pleasure.

'My son was very close to his mother. He and I are also close but I am so busy, always busy. We see little of each other.'

I had been wondering about Eneas's mother. Where was she? But I felt reluctant to ask about her. Perhaps there had been a divorce. Perhaps she was ill. Perhaps she was dead.

'Are things difficult in your hospital?'

'Difficult? How difficult?' José frowned.

'Well, I've heard that even the commonest medicines are in short supply. Aspirins, antibiotics, even vitamins.'

José gazed across the room, still frowning, for a moment in silence. Then he looked at me, scrutinising me as though for the first time, and sighed. Wearily he said: 'We have no shortages. We have all the drugs we need. Cuba has the best medical services in the whole of Latin America.'

'Yes, I know that. I just thought . . .'

The grandfather intervened: 'Perhaps you would like some more coffee?'

'Oh, no, thank you.' I knew that coffee, like everything else, was in extremely short supply in Cuba. 'If I drink any more coffee, I won't be able to sleep.' I bent down for my Harrods bag. 'Which reminds me. I have some coffee and tea here. And some other things.'

When I started taking one thing after another out of

the bag, the family were as embarrassed as I was. They muttered their thanks, they told me that this commodity would be very useful and that that commodity had been unobtainable except on the black market for more than a year.

To Alonso, in addition to the soap and dried milk, I gave a pair of cotton socks which I had intended for Eneas. I had originally bought them at Marks & Spencer not as a present but for myself. 'I need socks,' Alonso said simply. He held them up to the light in both his long, knobbly hands and examined them. Then he said: 'Good,' with a smile which revealed broken, yellow teeth and purple receding gums. 'Thank you. Thank you.'

Eventually, as conversation foundered, I guessed it was time for me to go. Eneas came with me out to the car. 'I am sorry if I cannot come back with you. But Alonso wishes to go on to see his sister on the other side of Havana and there will be no bus.'

'Of course you mustn't come back with me.'

As he opened the car door for me, he stooped and told me in a low, husky voice: 'Do not believe my father. It is not true that the hospital has all the drugs which are necessary. Many people in Cuba are going blind for lack of vitamins.'

I wanted to ask Eneas why José had lied to me – out of fear? out of patriotism? – but there was no chance to do so, since Alonso had started up the engine.

'That was a wonderful evening.'

'Did you really enjoy it?'

'Yes, of course. Of course! I so much liked your family. And I'm glad you showed me your room.'

He gripped my hand in his. Then he once more threw

his arms around me, hugging me close. *It means nothing, it means nothing, nothing at all.* But I wanted, I so much wanted to believe that it did.

As I stepped out of the car outside the hotel, a policeman in uniform approached and beckoned Alonso to step out of it as well. The two men, the one white, young and erect and the other black, old and bowed, confronted each other. After they had talked for a while, Alonso sighed, drew his wallet out of the breast pocket of his tattered jacket and produced some papers from it. Then he noticed me standing a few feet away.

'It is all right. You need not wait. It is nothing. A formality.'

But I waited.

The policeman, totally ignoring my presence, shuffled through the papers, holding a torch up to them to do so. He asked Alonso some questions and Alonso answered in his slow, deep voice.

Eventually the policeman sauntered off.

'Is there some problem?'

'No, no problem. Except that in Cuba there is always a problem.' Alonso gave a crooked smile. 'Don't worry yourself. I – we – are used to such happenings.' He began to clamber back into the car. 'I will say goodbye.'

Suddenly I remembered the five dollars. I pulled them out of my pocket.

'I want to give you this. For the petrol – gasoline – and all your trouble.'

'But it's really not necessary ... I was happy ...'

'Of course it's necessary. Please!' I pressed the note into his palm. Then, on an impulse, I said: 'Eneas's mother – I expected to see her.'

'His mother? She is dead.' To my amazement, he crossed himself, head bowed, as he told me this.

'Dead?'

'Yes, she died last December – on Christmas Day. She had been ill for many years. Tuberculosis.'

'How sad!'

'Yes, very sad. Only forty-three. A beautiful and charming lady.' He turned away, then turned back. 'Well, we meet tomorrow. Is that right?'

Eneas had told me that Alonso could drive us for all the next day.

'If it's not too much trouble. If you can spare the time.'

'Of course! Of course!'

The gears grumbled fretfully as he engaged them. Then, with a loud, smoky fart, the huge, dilapidated car swerved into the centre of the road and was off.

# 10

The sun was setting over the purple humps of the distant mountains as we drove home from our excursion to Pinar del Rio. Suddenly Alonso peered at the petrol gauge, tapped it with a knuckle, peered at it again. He drew in his breath on a hiss and shook his head. 'What has happened to all the gas?'

Eneas leaned over to look. He asked Alonso something in Spanish and Alonso replied, in English: 'Ten, fifteen kilometres. But maybe they have nothing. Usually I have a spare can. I am a fool, a fool! I forgot that I used it last week.'

As we drove on, I could see how anxious the Cubans were becoming. Probably they were worrying more about me than themselves. If we were stranded and had to flag down one of the few trucks which thundered down the highway, how would I react to having to perch on a mound of sugar-cane or of yams in the rear? But I myself felt none of this anxiety. My mood was one of cheerful stoicism. When one is totally happy, what would otherwise be a mishap becomes merely 'an adventure' or 'fun'.

Eventually we reached the next village. The yard of

the tiny petrol station was deserted except for a hen and three chicks scratching around in the dust. After repeated shouting, Eneas managed to summon the yawning, bleary-eyed attendant in grubby overalls and canvas shoes trodden down at the heels from the shack to which he must have prematurely retreated for an early night.

Dolefully, the attendant shook his head – no petrol, it was clear.

Alonso and Eneas began to argue with him, gesticulating more and more vehemently, their voices growing louder and louder. Then Eneas trotted over to the car, in which I had remained. He poked his head through the open window and in a low voice – surely unnecessary, since it was unlikely that the attendant spoke any English? – said: 'I am sorry, I am very sorry. But have you any dollars?'

'Yes, of course.' I fumbled for my wallet. 'Why?'

'He says that there is no gas. No gas for a week. But if he is given dollars – I think that maybe we have a miracle.'

'How much do you want?'

'Twenty?' In his humiliation Eneas looked angry. 'I am sorry. I am very sorry.'

'Don't be silly.'

'I wish I could repay you.'

'One day perhaps you will.'

As we drove off again, the grinning attendant raising an arm in farewell, I could not resist asking Eneas: 'Does everyone in the police force use the *mercado negro*?' I had learned the Spanish phrase from him. Then I wished that I had not put the question. I wanted to know the answer; but, whatever it was, it could only embarrass and humiliate him.

For a few seconds he was silent. Had he failed either

to hear me or to understand me? Or had he decided to ignore the question? Then he gave a grimace, as though he had sucked on something sour. 'Of course.' He shrugged as though to say: What a foolish thing to ask.

He was right. It was a foolish thing.

Soon after that, an old woman in a long, shapeless dress, a kerchief tied about her head and a basket in either hand, appeared ahead of us in the dimming light of evening. As the car chugged towards her, she lowered one of the baskets and stepped out into the road, raising her arm.

Alonso swerved past her and began to drive on. Eneas said something in Spanish and both of them laughed.

'Oh, do let's give her a lift!'

Both men ignored me.

'Please!'

Eneas sighed and then leaned forward and spoke to Alonso. The car began to slow down and eventually halted. Looking back through the cracked rear window, I could see the old woman loping towards us in a cloud of dust. Her kerchief was coming loose, one end trailing in the wind.

Gasping for breath and muttering 'Gracias! Gracias!', she clambered into the seat beside Alonso. Then she began to laugh, a high-pitched whinny. Clearly, she could not believe her luck. From one of her baskets she took out a bunch of bananas. She handed one banana to Alonso, who placed it in the glove-compartment beside him, one to Eneas, who at once began to peel it and eat it, and one to me, who held it, uncertain what to do with it. Only I thanked her.

For a few minutes she was silent, her head nodding in

[94]

front of me, so that I assumed that she must have fallen asleep. Then, all at once, she was talking, talking on and on, in the same high, loud voice, almost as though she were reciting some speech long since learned. From time to time one of the others would interject something, a stone thrown into the rushing stream of her story. But the stone could not divert, much less halt, the stream as irresistibly it carried all before it.

At last she fell silent. She broke off a banana from the bunch, tore back now one strip and now another of its peel, and placed its end in her mouth. She sucked on it, like a child on a lollipop, before at last biting into it.

Eneas turned to me: 'She has a strange story,' he said. 'Very strange.' All at once I realised that this strange story must have disturbed or excited him. His eyes, under their thick, beautifully arched eyebrows, looked unnaturally large, his nostrils were dilated.

'It is all nonsense,' Alonso turned his head to say. 'Peasant nonsense.'

'Perhaps.' Eneas was clearly not convinced.

'What is it? Tell me what she said.'

Eneas hesitated.

'Yes?'

He squirmed uneasily, his body still pressed so close to mine that I almost felt it to be part of my own. 'She lives over there.' He pointed towards the distant mountains, now looking like piles of coal from which the last glow of the sun was beginning to expire. 'Far away. Many kilometres.'

'How did she get to where we picked her up?'

The question did not interest him. 'Maybe she walked. Maybe someone gave her *autostop*.' He shrugged. Then in a low, puzzled voice he said: 'Strange things happen in her village.'

[95]

'Strange? Tell me.'

Again there was that long silence. Hands clasped in his lap and lower lip drawn between his teeth, he gazed out of the window beside him.

'Tell me.'

Between them, he and Alonso then told the story. The old woman's village lay in a deep gash between one mountain and another. There were caves there, innumerable caves, some of them never explored to their full extent. During the revolution, some of Batista's men, having been hunted across the plain, had eventually holed up in one of those caves. Castro's men had found them and had burned them all to death, piling up brushwood in the entrance, dousing it with petrol and then igniting it.

Now, in that same cave, just a cave like any other of the caves, three children from the village, perfectly ordinary children, not particularly well educated, not particularly bright, not particularly religious, had had a vision of the Virgin Mary.

At this point, Alonso laughed. But Eneas was grave.

The Virgin Mary had given them a message, which they had passed on to the local priest.

'And has the priest passed on this message to others?'

Eneas shook his head. 'She says not.'

'Why not?'

'He is frightened.'

'Frightened? What of?'

'She does not know. No one knows. Maybe . . .' He broke off.

'Yes?'

He remained silent.

'How odd!' I exclaimed, half interested and half irritated.

[96]

Alonso once again turned round. 'Superstition, just superstition. In such villages nothing happens. People are born, people work their land, people make love, people die. Nothing else, nothing, nothing. So they are bored. So they make an excitement for themselves.'

After that, all of us fell silent.

Then, suddenly, the old woman began to sing, in a piercingly high, tremulous voice, her eyes closed and her head tilted backwards. In Senegal, many years before, I had heard an old woman in a village in the jungle sing a lullaby like that, her grandchild or great-grandchild resting across her knees as she had squatted before the mud hut in which, presumably, she and her family all lived crowded together. On that previous occasion, there had been something soothing and consoling about the singing. But now it struck me as eerie.

Lips pursed, Eneas looked upset by the sound.

Then, the pitch gliding down to a note an octave lower, the old woman broke off. When, a few moments later, I peered round the seat in front of me to look at her, I saw that she had fallen asleep.

'Was that a folk-song?'

Neither of the men answered. Perhaps they did not know.

A few miles outside Havana, with no sign of any habitation, the woman opened her eyes and started up in her seat. She said something urgent in Spanish and Alonso brought the car to a shuddering halt.

'She wishes to get out,' Eneas told me.

'*Here?* But there's not a single house in sight.'

'Maybe she has a long walk.' He seemed totally indifferent to her fate. Having scrambled out of the car, the woman leaned through the window, extending a claw. I shook it and then, with obvious reluctance, Eneas did so.

[97]

'*Gracias! Gracias!*' She turned; looked about her, as though she were lost or had to get her bearings; then began to trudge back the way we had come.

Suddenly, opening the door beside him, Eneas was calling out to her. She halted, a basket in either hand, her body leaning forward. He asked her some question. Extraordinarily loud, as though magnified by some hidden microphone, her voice came back with the answer.

'*Gracias, señora!*' Eneas shouted to her again retreating figure.

'What did you ask her?'

'The name of her village.'

Why should he want to know the name of her village?

# 11

The next day, as Eneas sat opposite to me in an open-air café, his long athlete's legs outstretched before him, I noticed that the sole of one of his canvas shoes had a hole in it. I pointed.

'Yes, yes!' He raised his foot and peered down at the hole. 'What am I to do? There are no shoes in the shops. There is nothing in the shops. You have seen yourself.' That morning, walking through old Havana, I had peered into shop-windows totally devoid of goods. Many shops were closed, some were even boarded up.

'Let me buy you some new shoes.'

'No.'

'Why not?'

'*No!*'

'Oh, come on! Shoes don't cost all that much. We can go to one of the dollar shops. Why not? You can't walk around in those shoes, the dust must get into them.'

We argued for a while; then, sulkily, as though he were consenting to do me a favour which he did not really wish to do, he gave in.

There were no shoes in the hotel shop where I had bought the soap, dried milk, Nescafé and tea.

'Where else can we go?'

Eneas shrugged.

'Isn't there somewhere else?'

Eventually, with extreme reluctance, he said that in Miramar, where most of the embassies and embassy residences were situated, there was a large store open only to diplomats – and tourists who could be mistaken for diplomats.

'Do you think that I could be mistaken for a diplomat?'

'Of course!'

No one attempted to bar our entry. Eneas tried on shoe after shoe, for far longer than I had ever seen any man do before. From time to time, he would ask my opinion: did I like the colour, did I think that this pair looked too cheap, wasn't this toe far too narrow? At long last, he found what he wanted.

'Are they too expensive?'

'No, of course not.'

The prolonged act of helping to choose the shoes, which would certainly have bored and exasperated me if I had had to do it for anyone else, had filled me with excitement.

I then paid for the shoes, after which the sales assistant placed them in a box and, taking many minutes to do so, made a neat parcel of them in brown paper and string. Once the transaction was complete, I said: 'And now I'm going to buy you some trousers.'

'No. No!' Once again, as when I had first suggested the purchase of the shoes, Eneas sounded indignant, almost angry.

'Yes, I insist. I saw some very nice ones in linen over there.' I pointed. I had noticed that, whenever we met, he was always wearing the same pair of jeans. Such threadbare jeans might be regarded as the height of fashion in London; they were certainly not so in Cuba.

'You have spent too much money already. Far too much.'

For a while we argued in an aisle of the store, with other shoppers constantly pushing past us. Then, as with the shoes, he gave in with a resigned sigh and a sulky: 'As you wish.'

Once more, he spent minutes on end inspecting what was on offer on the racks. Wasn't this blue far too bright? Didn't this cloth look cheap? Did I like turn-ups? By now my excitement had become a sexual one.

'You'd better try them on to see if they fit you.'

Eneas asked an assistant for a changing-room. Learning there was none, he unselfconsciously unzipped his jeans and stepped out of them, in only his Y-fronts, and then handed the jeans to me. None of the other shoppers seemed to be in the least surprised. I watched him avidly.

'What do you think?' The trousers were on. Like a model, he strutted towards me, pirouetted, strutted away from me.

'Perfect. They look perfect. But are you comfortable in them?'

'Yes, yes. Very comfortable.'

Again, as I paid, he protested that the trousers were too expensive; and again I told him not to be silly, I wanted to buy them for him, I enjoyed buying them for him.

*I enjoyed buying them for him.* Never before had I experienced such delight at spending money on somebody else. I felt intoxicated with it. I felt an extraordinary upsurge of energy and joy. I might have just snorted some of that fine ash offered to me in the ramshackle Oldsmobile.

When we left the shop, Eneas put an arm around my shoulders. 'You are too good!'

I wanted to say: 'It's not goodness that makes me be generous to you.'

But I merely muttered: 'Oh, don't be silly.'


That same evening, during dinner back at the hotel, Eneas began to ask me about all the countries to which I had travelled.

'But you have been everywhere, everywhere!'

'No, I'm afraid not. I've never visited China or Thailand or Hawaii – oh, a lot of places.'

'I have never left Cuba.'

'Would you be allowed to leave?'

He was doubtful. 'Maybe. If I have an invitation.'

'Well, why can't I give you an invitation?'

'You?' He was astonished.

'Why not? I could pay your fare. And you could live for nothing in my house. I have a guest-room – in fact, I have two guest-rooms. Oh, Eneas, do think about it. It's a wonderful idea!'

For a brief moment he shared my excitement; then his face stiffened. He shook his head. 'Yes, it is my dream to travel. But now – I cannot leave Cuba.'

'You mean that they wouldn't give you extended leave from your job? Surely, if you told them that you wanted to improve your English, they'd be – '

'No, no! It is not my job. But now – at this time – every Cuban should stay in Cuba. That is important, very important.'

'But why, why?'

He stared at me, with what seemed a resentful incredulity. Then he reiterated: 'That is important, very important.'

# 12

Two days later, as we once again lay out side by side on the beach – Alonso was sprawled some distance away from us, sucking contemplatively on a huge cigar, his back against the trunk of a dead tree – Eneas began to talk of his mother.

Before that, he had been speaking of his father – how he loved him and admired him but how the two of them were too different from each other ever to be really close. Then, abruptly sitting up, he scooped up a handful of sand and let it trickle through his fingers. With his mother, it had been different, he said. They had been close, close. They were so like each other.

He began to speak of her prolonged illness: the fevers, the spells in sanatoria, the alternations between hope and despair, the stays up in the mountains, the haemorrhages, the last of which had taken place when he and she had been alone in the house together. 'She was ironing my shirt. She began to cough. Then blood, blood, much blood, blood everywhere.'

On an impulse, to comfort him, I put out a hand and, after a moment of hesitation, rested it on his bare back. I stroked the back, then left the hand there. He did not shift away.

'She did not need to die,' he said.

'What do you mean?'

'If she had had enough food . . . If we could have given her the right medicines . . .'

'One can't be sure of that.'

He slammed his hand down into the sand between his feet. 'This fucking country!'

Where had he learned that word? Jealousy briefly but agonisingly transfixed me. Perhaps there had been another foreign friend, some English or Canadian tourist, before me. Perhaps he was not nearly as innocent as he seemed.

'This fucking, fucking country!'

All at once he was sobbing. His face looked ugly then, the mouth contorted, the eyes screwed up, a thread of saliva on his chin glistening in the sunlight. His body shook. Wild, gulping noises came from him.

I shifted my hand from his back to his shoulder, patted the shoulder, patted it again.

Suddenly, with a grunt that was almost a growl, he jerked himself away from me. Then he jumped to his feet and raced down the long, gradual incline of burning sand to the sea. He hurled himself into it and swam out and out and out, until, squinting into the glare, I could scarcely see him.


That had been a long day. We had swum repeatedly, we had hired a small boat and had sailed in a circle of the wide bay. In the afternoon we had driven up into the hills and, leaving Alonso and the car, had followed a footpath, zigzagging up and up, until we had a view of

[104]

the whole of Havana vaporous in the accumulated heat and dust of the fiery afternoon.

When, soon after seven, we returned to the city, Eneas looked grey with fatigue.

'Where shall we go and eat?'

'Forgive me. I am tired. I think that maybe I go home now.'

'Oh! Oh, really?' I tried to conceal my disappointment but, greedy as I was for his company, I could not do so.

He touched my arm. In a strangely soft, beseeching, almost wheedling voice, he asked: 'You are not angry?' He might have been a child speaking to its parent.

'No, no. Of course not! Go home and have a good night's sleep.'

Now holding my arm, he peered into my face. Then he burst into laughter: 'You are not tired! You are not tired at all.'

Truthfully I could answer: 'No, I'm not tired. Not at all tired. I don't know why, but I'm not. It must be the air of Havana. Or your company,' I added. 'When I'm with you . . .' I broke off.

'What will you do now?'

'Oh, I'll have some dinner in the hotel. And then – oh, then I may just wander through the city.'

'Take care!'

'Yes, I'll take care.'

# 13

That Sunday Eneas had insisted that I come out to his home for lunch.

Alonso was not free and so I hired a dollar taxi. No, no, I had told Eneas, there was no need for him to go to all the trouble of waiting on and on for a bus in order to come and fetch me; I was sure that the taxi-driver could find the address.

Fortunately, after some indecision, I had put on a suit and tie, since I found the whole family obviously dressed in their best for the occasion. Eneas was wearing the linen trousers which I had bought him and a silk shirt, once mine, which I had insisted on his taking when he had told me how much he liked it.

Fortunately, too, I had brought with me a bottle of rum and a bottle of Argentinian wine from the shop at the hotel. When I presented both to José, his narrow, saturnine face relaxed in a smile of gratitude and relief. 'I was worrying that there was nothing for you to drink,' he said. 'I mean, no alcohol.'

'It wouldn't have mattered.'

'But Eneas has told us that you like to drink with every meal.'

Once again we sat in a circle, with Eneas outside it. José poured out rum for his father, for me, for himself. He poured out none for his mother or Eneas. He raised his glass: 'Cheers!' Then, without drinking from it, he lowered it and asked: 'Is that what you say in England?'

I nodded and raised my glass: 'Cheers!'

José put his glass to his lips. 'Havana Club 7. Good, good!' His eyes, usually so dull beneath their dark, creased lids, now actually sparkled.

'It is a long, long time since my father drank Havana Club 7,' Eneas said. 'Now Havana Club 7 is only for tourists. Do you know that, for Cubans, there is a ration of rum? Half one bottle each month.'

José scowled at his son; then, obviously eager to change the subject, he turned back to me: 'You have visited our China Town? No? You must make Eneas take you there. It is very interesting.'

Soon Eneas and his grandmother had disappeared into the back of the house. I talked on with the two older men.

At one point, in one of the frequent pauses in our conversation, the grandfather announced: 'Today we are eating lobster. Black market lobster!' He threw back his head and guffawed. Once again José scowled. 'Everything we eat today is from the *mercado negro*. Because you are here, we are making a festival. Do you like lobster?'

Now I was faced with a terrible quandary. They must certainly have spent a lot of money and they had probably taken a risk in buying from the black market. But I have a life-long allergy to shell-fish. Was I to tell them or was I to make myself extremely ill? I hesitated.

'I'm terribly sorry . . . I – I just can't eat lobster. All my life I've had an allergy to it.'

The two men stared at me in consternation.

[107]

'You cannot eat lobster?' the old man asked, incredulous.

Miserably I shook my head. 'But don't worry, please don't worry. It doesn't matter. I can eat anything else.' I forced a smile. 'Or nothing. I've been eating far too much in Cuba. It'll be good for me to fast.'

'There is no need to fast,' José said severely. 'We have bread, salad, beans. But this is unfortunate, very unfortunate. Why didn't Eneas tell us?'

'Because he didn't know. I never had occasion to tell him.'

Eventually, while I struggled to get through a high-piled plate of *moros y cristianos*, the others devoured the lobster. Clearly they had eaten nothing so good for a long, long time. Even José's tense, mournful face relaxed and brightened. 'This is wonderful, mother,' the old man told his wife in English. Guessing what he was saying, she nodded vigorously while cracking a claw between her teeth. Eneas's face, lowered over his plate, was sweaty and flushed with the exertion. Now there was no conversation and the only sounds were of the smashing of the casings about the pinkish-white flesh and of a strenuous munching and sucking.

José kept pouring out rum for me, for himself, for his father. His mother got none, Eneas only a single glass. At one point he apologised for the absence of ice. They had no refrigerator; once they had had one but, more than thirty years old, it had eventually expired. The iceman had failed to come. No doubt he had been unable to get petrol for his van.

The whole family were somnolent once the long meal was over. In addition to the lobster, they had stuffed salad into their mouths; had chewed on hunks of bread dipped in olive oil, which had then dribbled down their

[108]

chins; had helped themselves to serving after serving of the white and black beans. The old man had belched repeatedly, making no attempt at concealment. The old woman had bitten dèep into a hard, unpeeled pear, her teeth crunching on it.

'You have eaten so little,' José complained to me.

'Oh, no! I've eaten far too much. Those beans were wonderful.' Already my stomach felt uncomfortably swollen with them.

'Let us finish this rum.' Despite my protest, he slopped some more into my glass. Then he sighed: 'I do not feel like going to the hospital.'

'Do you have to go today?'

Wearily he nodded. 'Even on Sunday people need emergency operations. I start duty at five.'

'Let me give you a lift in the taxi which is coming to take me back to the hotel.'

'No, no. It's too far. It will be too expensive for you. I can go on my bicycle. I am used to my bicycle.'

At that moment there was a ring and then a knock at the door. All of them looked at each other in alarm. Then José signalled to Eneas to go and see who it was.

On the doorstep was a woman so tiny that at first I mistook her for a child. Her head was covered in a tangled mass of grey curls, some tumbling over her forehead and almost into her eyes. She was wearing a shift-like dress, its hem sagging at one side, which looked as if she must have been sleeping rough in it for days and days on end. Her legs were bare, with bruise-like discolourations on them. There were straw slippers on her feet.

Without waiting for Eneas or anyone else to invite her in, she marched towards the table at which we were sitting. Having greeted everyone – the two men pushed

[109]

back their chairs and lurched to their feet – she looked at me. She pointed. When she spoke, I realised that she was asking whether I was the Englishman.

Yes, yes, José replied, I was Eneas's friend – *el amigo de Eneas*.

Grinning to display two or three crooked, brownish-yellow teeth, she held out a dirt-seamed hand for me to shake. Then in English she said: 'Everything okay?'

I nodded.

'*Bueno! Bueno!*' Now she swung round to the old woman. Hearing the word '*langosta*', I understood that she was asking if the lobster had been good.

The old woman nodded her head vigorously. '*Sí, sí! Magnifico!*'

The other three now joined in – everything had been *perfecto, acabado, excelente*. Repeatedly they thanked her.

Next I understood her to ask whether we needed anything else.

No, no, everything was fine, we needed nothing more. There were more smiles, more expressions of gratitude.

The woman moved closer to me. By then, following the example of the others, I too had got to my feet. She put out a hand and, suddenly and painfully, grasped in it what my mother used to call my 'spare tyre'. She grinned. *Hermoso*, she told me – beautiful. She looked around at the others. She repeated the *hermoso*, still gripping the flabby flesh. Was she making a joke? Was she trying to humiliate me? Then I realised that she was doing neither of these things, she was paying me a compliment. The others were all nodding. In a country where people live in a state of near-starvation, to be fat is an indication of power and wealth and therefore, like those two things, exerts an attraction.

After she had gone, the others hastened to tell me who

[110]

she was. It was she who had provided the lobster, the oil, the bread, the fruit, the lettuce, tomato and onion for the salad. She was the queen of the *mercado negro* in their district.

She was rich, rich, the old man said. Richer than any of their neighbours.

A dollar millionairess, said Eneas.

José shook his head, irritated. No, that was an exaggeration. But she had certainly accumulated a lot of dollars.

Yet she lived in a hovel, said the old man. One would be ashamed to keep a dog in it. I could see for myself how she dressed and how dirty she was.

She couldn't spend any money, Eneas took up. If she did, she would betray what she was doing. She was waiting, waiting patiently. She was hoping that one day, with a change of government, she would be able to buy herself a mansion, a car, a television set, beautiful clothes. But now she lived in constant fear that the police would discover her activities and haul her off to gaol.

I wanted to ask Eneas why, in that case, she was not afraid of him, a policeman. But I did not wish to embarrass him. In that society in which everyone who wished to survive had to be in some way, however ambiguous, corrupt, perhaps she was not afraid of Eneas because she had squared him. Had the lobster been a gift or cost less than it would otherwise have cost? Had she provided some other commodity for the family in the past? Might it be she who produced the fuel which Alonso needed to drive us around in that petrol-guzzling car of his?

'She is a bad woman,' José concluded.

'But without her most people in this quarter would be dying or dead,' the old man put in.

[111]

José shook his head vigorously.

'*Sí! Sí!*' the old man protested, and his wife, as though she had been able to follow the conversation, mouthed an inaudible '*Sí!*' in echo. Behind her, Eneas nodded.

# 14

Eneas had announced to me that he was going to take me to the Coppelia. It was an ice-cream parlour, he had explained, where everyone, yes everyone, old or young, male or female, rich or poor, went to eat ice-creams, the best ice-creams in the whole of Cuba, perhaps in the world, and to meet other people. 'I can pay with peso. I wish to buy ice-cream for you. You have bought so many things for me, too many things. You make me ashamed.'

I had not told him that I did not like ice-creams. I had merely nodded and said: 'Thank you. That sounds terrific.'

When we stepped out of our taxi, I at once saw the queues, not two or three but at least a dozen, snaking back through the park and even spilling out into the road.

'We must wait,' Eneas said disconsolately, walking towards one of them.

Hadn't he known that there would be these queues? Probably he had, but to a Cuban they were so much a part of daily life that he must have thought nothing of it.

'How long do you think we'll have to wait?'

He shrugged and pulled a face. I knew what he was

thinking: *This has been a mistake. He's not used to queuing, as we are.*

The queue which we had joined seemed hardly to move. Indeed, every queue seemed hardly to move. But no one seemed to mind. Animatedly, the people chatted to each other. A boy in one queue would call out to a girl in another; after making contact, one or other of them would then cross over.

Eventually I pointed: 'That queue seems to be moving very fast.'

Eneas stared across, frowning. 'That is the queue for tourists. Dollar queue.'

Of course I should have left it at that. But, my back and calves aching from standing for so long and sweat dripping off my chin and the end of my nose – our queue had now crawled into a patch of blazing sunlight – I said: 'Why don't we join it?'

Irritably Eneas replied: 'Because I have only peso.'

'Well, I have dollars.' He said nothing, turning his head away. 'My dollars are your dollars. Let's get out of this queue and spend them. Eneas!' There was no reaction, his head still turned away. *'Eneas!'*

Without saying a word, he began to stride towards the tourist queue. Relieved but also ashamed, I followed him. In front of us there were now some young Canadians, girls and boys, chattering and laughing; a middle-aged couple, either Spanish or Latin American; and an elderly woman, on her own, who could have come from any country in Europe. Within minutes we were seated at a table; and within a few more minutes our ice-creams were before us. I dipped in my spoon. These might be the best ice-creams in Cuba, but to me the synthetic flavour of banana was nauseating. Since bananas grew in the country, why didn't they use them?

[114]

Eneas was saying nothing, his face was expressionless. As he dug his spoon into the mound of chocolate and coffee ice, he heaved a deep sigh.

'Don't be angry, Eneas. It was the best thing to do. I know you wanted to treat me but it would have been foolish to have waited there for an hour, two hours, when by spending a few dollars – '

At that, in a harsh, indignant voice, such as I had never heard him use before, he cut in: 'Those people may wait not for one hour or two hours but for three hours, four hours.'

'Yes . . . It's dreadful.'

We went on eating in silence. Then, all at once, he looked over to me and gave me the sweetest of smiles. The thunderous mood had passed.

'You like your ice-cream?'

'Wonderful,' I lied.

'I said – the best in Cuba.' He twisted round in his chair and pointed out of the huge window behind him. 'They are happy to wait. They talk, talk. Boy meets girl.'

'Have you met girls there?'

He threw back his head, he laughed delightedly. 'Many times, many, many times.'

It was after we had finished our ice-creams and were waiting, waiting on and on, for the harassed waitress to bring us glasses of mineral water, that he suddenly said: 'There is something I wish to do tomorrow. Maybe you will think it strange but I wish to do it.'

'What is it?'

Putting his head close to mine and lowering his voice – who could hear us, unless that area was bugged? – he said that he had decided that he wanted to visit the village of which that old woman to whom we had given a lift four days before had told us. I remembered, didn't

[115]

I? The village in which those three children had had their vision of the Virgin Mary.

'Are you religious?'

At the question he wriggled in his chair, kicked out a leg and pulled in his chin. Then he replied hesitantly: 'My mother . . . she believed, believed very much.'

He went on to tell me that he had been talking to a cousin of his, a priest, about what had happened, or what was supposed to have happened, in that village. The cousin had heard the story already, many people had heard it. But there was nothing about it in the papers and no one spoke of it openly.

Why?

To that naive question of mine, he gave no answer.

Now he wanted to go to the village, to find out what had happened, what had *really* happened. The priest cousin also wanted to go. Would I go with them?

'Is Alonso going to drive us?'

He shook his head. 'Busy. He must take his wife to the hospital.' But the priest had a car – small, small, old, not comfortable – and he could drive us. The only problem was that he would need some dollars for the gas. At the mention of the dollars, Eneas looked rueful and ashamed.

'Well, I can give him those,' I said, thinking: So even a priest uses the *mercado negro*.

Eneas was relieved. 'You are a good man,' he said, not for the first time. 'I think that the visit will be interesting.'

'Yes, I think so too.'

When we left the park, the queues were even longer than before, and the chatter and laughter even louder. No one seemed exhausted or exasperated by the endless wait. All at once Eneas was buoyant. He grabbed my arm, put his mouth next to my ear and began to sing, in a nasal parody of an American accent: 'Everyone's a winner, baby, that's for sure.'

Where had he heard that ancient pop song? And did he really believe it? By then my own experience of life had convinced me that most people are losers, that's for sure.

# 15

How could a man of at least fifty-five be Eneas's cousin? He must be some more distant relation. Nonetheless, I could see a family resemblance between his battered, bloated face – the faces of alcoholics often have that kind of blurred, congested look – and Eneas's handsome one; and, despite the pot belly and the sloping shoulders, he too must once have had the physique of an athlete. There was no indication that he was a priest. Like Eneas, like almost every other Cuban man, he was dressed in jeans and a tee-shirt. Unlike Eneas, unlike almost every other Cuban man, he looked plump and prosperous.

'Do you speak English?' I asked him.

The priest, who was called Diego, examined me quizzically with eyes that were red-rimmed and slightly bleary before he replied: 'Yes, I speak English – though probably not as well as you would wish.' In fact, accent apart – I had heard Puerto Ricans pronounce English in exactly the same way – he spoke impeccably. Later, I was to learn that he had worked for many years as a missionary in Africa.

At first everything that he said to me seemed to be snide. 'I'm afraid you'll find this little car not at all to your taste'; 'I had to spend twelve of your dollars on the gas – maybe not a lot of money to you but a lot of money to us'; 'No, you needn't worry about the seat-belt, this is too uncivilised a country for anyone to worry about such things.' There were a number of remarks of that kind, each secreting, I persuaded myself, its corrosive venom. But I was determined not to be rattled or riled by them.

It was only when I handed round a packet of chocolate biscuits bought from the shop at the hotel – by then we had been travelling over the bumpy, dusty road for more than an hour – that his attitude to me changed. 'Eneas was lucky to meet you,' he told me, suddenly affable.

'I was lucky to meet him.'

'He has told me about the things that you have bought for him – the shoes, the trousers, so many things. He tells me that you are even going to buy him a camera.'

I felt acutely embarrassed. I wished that Eneas had said nothing about the presents. What inference might a man clearly so much more worldly than the rest of the family have drawn from them?

Diego began to talk of his experiences in Africa. For eleven years he had worked in a leper colony, where there had been American, Italian, French, Irish and English priests. 'Our lingua franca was English,' he explained. Then, to my surprise he began to speak of Graham Greene and his *A Burnt-Out Case*. Had I ever met Greene? No, I hadn't, I replied. He'd have liked to have met him, Diego said. Greene used to say that he was a Roman Catholic agnostic. What exactly did I think that he had meant by that?

Eneas, in the back of the Lada, was silent through all this. I began to wish that I was sitting beside him, instead of here in front where Diego had insisted that I sit. I began to wish that I was talking to Eneas in his halting

[119]

English about mundane things, instead of to Diego in his fluent English about intellectual ones.

We turned off the main road and took a rough, winding track up into the hills. It must, I decided, have been at the turn-off just past the one at which the old woman had flagged us down.

'I pray to God we don't have a puncture.'

'I'm sure God will answer the prayer of a priest.'

Without a smile, his massive shoulders hunched over the wheel, Diego continued to peer out through the windscreen with those red-rimmed, bleary eyes of his.

Suddenly I was thirsty. 'Would anyone like a drink?'

'What have you got?'

'Well, I brought some mineral water. I've now learned always to do that. And I've also got some Havana Club 7. Eneas told me that that's the best rum in the world.'

'I'll settle for the rum.' Diego's decision did not surprise me. He looked like a man who would always rather settle for alcohol than for water.

As we sat by the roadside, the other two on a fallen tree-trunk and I on a rock so sharp that I kept shifting uneasily on it, I said: 'I bought some tins in the shop. And I stole some rolls from the breakfast buffet. Any takers?'

Eneas grinned. 'I am hungry.'

I walked back to the car and brought out the Harrods bag which the black boy had tried to steal. 'Spam, tuna, sardines? Which is it to be?'

Eneas opted for tuna after I had explained what the three things were. I took out my Swiss penknife and opened the tin. At the shop I had also managed to find some paper plates and plastic spoons. I scooped out a portion of tuna on to one of the plates and handed it to

[120]

Diego. He pulled a face: 'I'm not sure I really want to eat any tuna.'

'Would you like something else?'

'Perhaps just some more rum.' I had already given him a generous measure. Was it wise to give him another equally generous when he was driving over such difficult terrain? Reluctantly I passed him the bottle.

'May I see?' Eneas put out his hand for the penknife. I passed it over to him and, with the wondering eagerness of a small boy, he then began to open it up. What was this for? And this? And this? 'Oh, that's for getting stones out of horses' hooves,' I told him at one moment. This added to his amazement.

Eventually he held out the penknife to me. 'I have never seen such a thing. Wonderful!'

'Keep it.'

He shook his head, uncomprehending.

'I'll give it to you. It's yours.'

'No, no!' He tried to make me take it back, pressing it into my obstinately closed fist and then trying to prise the fist open, laughing as he did so.

'Keep it. I can easily get another back in England. They're quite cheap there.'

At last, reluctantly, Eneas slipped the penknife into his pocket. Then he gave a small, delighted smile.

Diego gulped again from the paper mug. He set it down, wiped the back of his hand over his large mouth with its full lower lip. He gazed at me, steadily, quizzically, cynically.

I thought: *He knows the score!*

He was far too worldly not to know it.

\*

[121]

All at once, as we approached the mountains, everything was dense and green around us. Not for the first time I wondered how people could be living on the verge of starvation in a country seemingly so fertile. After a moment of hesitation – he might resent such a comment from a foreigner – I told Diego what I had been thinking.

He sighed wearily. 'It's crazy, it's all crazy. The economy is totally mismanaged. No private agriculture is allowed, so the country people have no incentive to grow anything other than what is produced by the cooperatives for which they work. Do you know the story of Alonso?'

'Our driver, you mean? What story?'

Diego began to tell it. Except when he chauffered people illicitly in his car, Alonso was now retired. Behind his house, there was a large garden – or, rather, there had been a large garden, since it was now no longer a garden but merely a wilderness. I must have realised that fresh vegetables were virtually unobtainable in Cuba – except, Diego added bitterly, in the tourist hotels and restaurants and on the black market. Well, since he had nothing else to occupy him and since he was fond of gardening, Alonso had started to grow vegetables in his garden. These vegetables he had then sold to his neighbours. He had made a little money, the neighbours had had fresh vegetables for the first time for many, many months. Then, one day, the police had visited him. Did he realise that he was breaking the law? Private enterprise of that kind was strictly forbidden. If he continued to sell his vegetables, he would find himself in prison.

'So' – he shrugged – 'Alonso stopped growing vegetables except in one little corner of his land for himself and his family. The rest of the land now grows nothing but weeds.'

[122]

'How absurd!'

Diego laughed. 'Yes, absurd. An absurd but tragic example of what is happening all over Cuba. The garden of Cuba is becoming a waste land. No one can live on what it produces.'

At this moment Eneas interrupted our conversation by shouting excitedly: 'See! Caves! Caves!'

We were now driving up into the mountains. From time to time on either side of the precipitous road I could see gashes in the rock face, many of them half screened by vegetation cascading from above. Then I noticed that one of these gashes had been boarded over with rusty corrugated iron. Did people live in the caves? Yes, Diego said. Some people still lived in them. After all, they were cool. Then he added, with the old needling bitterness: 'Although they can't be as comfortable as your air-conditioned hotel.'

It was soon after this that the incident of the dog took place. The road was circling what was not so much a village as a settlement when, from the side of one of its tumble-down shacks, a wolf-like dog suddenly shot out. Teeth bared and shaggy, grey coat staring, it threw itself on to the bonnet of the car and then, as though sucked under by some irresistible force, vanished beneath it. Diego had already swerved once, when the dog had appeared. Now he had swerved again. It was that second swerve which must have brought one of the wheels over the dog. There was a terrible screech as the car juddered and bounced.

Seemingly unperturbed – we might have bumped over a pothole – Diego drove on.

I looked back through the window. Quivering on its side, the dog lay out in the middle of the road, grey on glaring white.

[123]

'Oughtn't we to stop?'

'What's the point?' Diego said. 'He must be dead – or near to dead. There's nothing we can do.'

'Perhaps he has *rabia*,' Eneas said. 'Dangerous.'

'And the owner could demand a lot of money from us – if there is an owner.'

As we continued on up to the pass ahead, Diego and Eneas chattered away to each other, but I sat silent. I felt sickened and frightened by the self-destructive frenzy with which the dog had thrown himself on to the car. There had been something unnatural, something demonic, about that self-destroying assault.

I wished that I had not placed the bottle of rum back in the boot. I could have done with a swig.

It was the twenty-fifth of March. Suddenly, mysteriously, I do not know why, the realisation came to me. I broke my long silence to ask: 'Is this the Feast of the Annunciation?'

'Yes,' Diego replied. 'That's right.'

'And is that why ...?'

'The church in the village is the church of Our Lady of the Annunciation. It was on the last Feast of the Annunciation that Our Lady appeared to the children. Now we shall see if She appears again to them.' He turned his head and smiled at me. 'What do you think?'

'I've no idea. What do *you* think?'

'I've no idea either. No idea at all.'


Although it was not yet two o'clock, dusk seemed to be closing in prematurely. All colour was bleeding out of the sky, so that it became first ashen, then livid. At the same time I was increasingly oppressed by feelings of confinement, of restlessness. I wanted to say 'Do you think we could stop for a moment?', but it was less than half an hour since our last stop for our picnic and I felt that I could not do so. I shifted in my seat and shifted again, making Diego turn to glance at me.

Then he peered out through the windscreen at the sky. It now bulged over us, ominously close. 'I think we're going to have a storm,' he said.

'*Extraño*,' Eneas said. 'There was a storm last time.'

'How do you know that? I never heard that,' Diego said.

'Someone told me – that old woman or someone.'

The gradient was now so steep and the hairpin bends so sharp that the car seemed to be constantly on the verge of refusing to climb any further. 'Pray God there's no puncture, no puncture,' Diego muttered under his breath.

'Pray God I'm not car-sick,' I said aloud.

'Is that likely?'

'It's been known to happen.' I was, in fact, beginning to feel queasy.

Before anything else in the village, I saw the tower of the church, soaring up between the trees around it, grey against the darker grey of the sky, looking in its smoothness as though it were made not of stone but of metal. For a place so small, it seemed to be extraordinarily large. It was only later that I learned that the impoverished village had once been a prosperous town, in the days of Spanish rule.

'We have arrived,' Diego said. 'Just before the storm.'

No one appeared to live on the outskirts. Many of the houses were empty, some had even collapsed, with a façade or even only a single wall rising above a pile of rubble. 'Has there been an earthquake here?' I asked.

'Only the revolution,' Diego replied sardonically.

[125]

A solitary woman halted, hand raised to forehead, and watched us as we chugged past. Dangling from her other wrist was a cord at the end of which a cockerel had been tied by its feet. I guessed that the bird must be alive, but from its total immobility it might have been dead.

Now there were more people about, some walking lethargically up what must be the main street, others seated on the wide steps of what I took to be some kind of municipal building, its bricks the colour of raw beef, its steeply sloping roof the colour of raw liver. A truck hurtled out of a side-street, almost colliding with us, and then, enveloping us in a cloud of acrid dust, screeched off ahead. People were packed into it. It was amazing that, with such a load, it could travel so fast.

'*Loco!*' Eneas shouted from behind me, his head stuck out of the window. The antiquated engine of the truck was making so much noise and we ourselves were making so much noise, grinding up the hill, that the truck-driver could not possibly have heard him.

'He lives next to the church,' Diego said. I guessed that 'he' was not the driver of the truck but the parish priest.

Eneas then said something in Spanish, presumably asking the priest's name, since Diego replied: 'Padre Antonio.'

On the steps of the gaunt church people were also seated, far, far more people than on the steps of the municipal building, all strangely motionless, all strangely silent. Beside the church, there was a house, obviously the oldest in the village, with rusty iron railings around a square of garden in which the blossoms of a number of towering bushes, cramped together in that small space, flared under the leaden sky. 'That must be his house,' Diego said. All the people on the steps were now staring at the car – which must then have been one of the few in

[126]

the whole village. Then, as I got out, I was uncomfortably aware that everyone was now staring not at the car but at me.

I looked nervously back at them, over my shoulder; then was blinded by a flash of lightning, which made me feel as if something extremely bright and sharp, the blade of a giant guillotine, had crashed down between me and those mute onlookers. Almost simultaneously, thunder boomed out and echoed on and on, back and forth from one side of the mountains to the other. Rain hissed on the roof of the car, as though on a heated grill.

'Run!' Diego urged, beginning to run himself. But the crowds on the steps made no effort to shelter, as they could easily have done inside the church. They sat there or stood there, still silent and motionless. As I began to run, I saw that from the truck, now parked diagonally to the church on a patch of mustard-coloured grass, people were jumping down. They, too, were strangely, ominously silent.

Father Antonio, appearing in the gloom behind the elderly woman who had opened the door, was like some tall, silver statue blotched with verdigris. In Cuba I had never seen a man, not even a young one, with hair so long. A silver mane, falling to his narrow, bony shoulders, it had a greenish tinge where its ends turned stiffly up, as though after the application of curling tongs. There was the same greenish tinge to his pebble glasses, to the hollows on either side of his forehead, to his cheekbones. There was also a greenish tinge, but one far darker, to his tattered, black robes.

He seemed vague, distracted, distant, as Diego told him who we were and why we had come. 'He says many people are coming,' Diego told me. 'The authorities have told Father Antonio that all this is superstition and that

[127]

he shouldn't encourage it. He may get into trouble. I hope not.'

Soon we were sitting in a small, bare room, on straight-backed wooden chairs. Father Antonio was not sitting but standing, his back against the wall to support a body so emaciated that I decided that he was suffering not merely from the usual lack of food but from some serious illness, perhaps a mortal one.

'What sort of trouble could he get into?' I asked.

Instead of answering, Diego turned away from me, impatiently it seemed, to put some question to our host.

'Soon we can meet the children. Then there will be a service in the church. Then we shall go to the cave,' Diego translated, when Father Antonio had given his answer in his faint, strangely high voice, the voice of a young girl issuing from the mouth of a man who must have been in his seventies or even eighties, to a question about the order of events.

By now I had again begun to feel an overwhelming thirst. In the boot of the car, there was still a bottle of mineral water. Should I go out and fetch it? Eventually, I whispered to Eneas: 'I feel parched. I must have something to drink.'

He waited for a while, head cocked on one side while the Father and Diego continued to converse together. Then he interrupted them.

The Father turned and called through the half-open door into the shadowy interior of the house. He then resumed what he was saying, not even breaking off when a plump young woman with a cruelly obvious hare-lip brought in the water. The glass was not on a tray but in her hand. She held it out to me. Even through the thick glass, the water felt warm, and it had a peculiar orange sheen to it. When I sipped, the taste was slightly bitter.

The Father must have noticed my look of distaste. He broke off to say something to Eneas, who then told me: 'There is no need to worry. The water comes from a spring in the garden. That colour is natural, not bad, no problem for you. All the water in the village has the same colour.'

I gulped and gulped again.

Monotonously the two voices went on and on. Most of the time Eneas merely listened, listened attentively, leaning forward on his chair, even from time to time tilting it, his muscular hands – such beautiful hands, I thought again, so scrupulously kept – clasped between his wide-open knees. I felt an inexorable sleepiness descend on me. Briefly lightning flashed across the small, darkening room from the window. Far off now, there was another boom of thunder. Then I closed my eyes.

I was woken by the sound of children's voices. There were three of them, and the girl with the hare-lip was ushering them into the room. Outside, in the hall beyond the door, there were three – no four – adults, three women and, almost invisible in a far corner as I peered round, a man. The women were middle-aged, ill-shapen, with sallow, tired faces; the man was older, red-faced, his lean, crooked body propped on a stick with a rubber ferrule. From all of them there seemed to pulse a feverish excitement. Suddenly I felt that excitement beginning to pulse within me too, just as a vibrating bell can set up a vibration in a bell near to it.

At first the children seemed to me nondescript. I had seen innumerable children exactly like them during my walks through those once elegant streets of Havana now reduced to squalid slums. Because of malnutrition such children were probably older than they seemed – twelve or thirteen or even fourteen, instead of eight or nine. The

[129]

only difference from those children of the slums was that these children, two girls and a boy, were wearing clean, white clothes, the girls the sort of frocks that might have been worn for a first communion, the boy in white shorts, reaching to almost below his knees, and a white shirt made of either silk or rayon. The girls' hair had been frizzed about their pallid, strangely worn faces; the boy's hair was naturally frizzy. Clearly the boy's ancestry was wholly or almost wholly African. The girls wore canvas shoes, as white as their dresses. The boy was barefoot, the toes widely splayed.

Suddenly I found myself staring at the boy, as he stood to attention, just as the girls were standing to attention, all their hands behind their backs, while Father Antonio's high-pitched voice lilted on and on, and out in the hall the four adults – parents or relatives of the children? – stood attentively silent.

Was it possible? Could this be the boy who had snatched at my bag and who, later, had shivered beside me in that police-car, with that ammoniac, repellent smell of terror oozing from his skinny body? Calmly the boy returned my gaze, held it, held it for seconds on end, his body motionless, his hands behind his back. Then he gave me the spectre of a smile, no more. *Yes, it's me, it's me!* Was that spectre of a smile really saying that? I did not know. I was never to know. Rationally it seemed then, as it seemed weeks and months later and even today, a total impossibility. How could a mere child have made that long journey from this village among the mountains to Havana? How could he have gained his release from prison – Eneas had told me that his trial would not take place for at least ten days – and returned home again? But, like a splinter, the doubt remained

embedded in my mind, irritating, dully throbbing, caus-
ing a slow suppuration, which is even now with me.

On and on they talked: mostly Father Antonio but now
also those parents and relatives – yes, the old man was
the father of one of the girls, one of the women was the
mother of the other of the girls, the other two women
were the boy's aunts, Diego told me – who crowded into
the doorway and then entered the room and finally began
to talk, at first hesitantly but then with increasing vehemence, that excitement previously pulsing within them at
last exploding into words, as the thunderstorm, so long
pent up within that heavily sagging sky, had at last
exploded into a deluge over the village and its visitors.

Neither Diego nor Eneas now bothered to translate for
me, unless I pressed them, asking insistently: 'What is he
saying?' or 'What was that? What was that?' The reason
was that they were themselves too absorbed, that feverish excitement now also pulsing irresistibly within them,
as it had pulsed within me.

By now, many voices were talking all at once. Only the
children, curiously detached, scarcely moving, said
nothing or almost nothing. I tried once more to catch the
eye of the boy but he refused to look at me.

At long last, we went out from the house, I unaccom-
panied in the train of the others, who were still gabbling
away. The children were way off in front.

To my amazement I found that the church square was
now thronged with people. They must have arrived,
in the antiquated buses, trucks and cars parked everywhere, in those two or three hours which we had spent
in the small, stuffy, bare room. Everyone was still and
silent as our party emerged from the house. But then,
when the crowd became aware of the children, a strange

[131]

noise swept through it; nothing articulate, no words, a kind of shushing and sighing like a wave sweeping slowly in on a beach and then withdrawing no less slowly.

The sky was clear now and, though it was past six, the light was strong enough to make me take my dark glasses out of the breast pocket of my jacket and put them on. I followed the others into the church. It irritated me that neither Diego nor Eneas should be in the least concerned about me, as they flanked Father Antonio, with the children ahead of them, purposefully marching, the girls linking their hands, the boy a footstep behind them, up the steps, through the throng, and into the church. At their silent passage, people jerked back, so that their bodies should have no contact with these other bodies. Were they afraid of contaminating or being contaminated? Did they feel reverence or a superstitious dread? There was no way to know.

Obeying a signal from Eneas – at last he had deigned to think of me! – I sat down in the front pew next to him. I felt embarrassed, as I always feel embarrassed on such occasions, at having been prevented by some scruple of conscience from crossing myself on entering the church, and I also felt an indefinable agitation, even terror. *What are you letting yourself in for?* All my life I have had a hatred and fear of the irrational.

The three children now stood before the altar, their hands again behind their backs and their faces expressing a kind of sweet, sorrowful composure. Behind, people were crowding in. A large woman thrust herself into the pew beside me, her irresistible bulk forcing my body yet closer to Eneas's. Her thick, long black dress – could she be wearing wool in this sultry heat? – must have been drenched by the rain. It was clammy against my knee; a smell, like the smell of a wet horse, wafted from it.

In that high, girlish voice, Father Antonio began to address the congregation. Now he seemed to be talking to them, now to be chanting to them. Sweat slithered down his forehead and into an eye. With an impatient gesture he raised a hand, pushed up his pebble glasses on to the sharp bridge of his nose, and brushed the sweat away. Everyone was totally motionless, except for myself. I shifted in my seat, once again shaken by the overwhelming restlessness which I had suffered in the car.

After many minutes, Father Antonio said something to the children. As though drilled, they then took a pace forward, exactly the same pace at exactly the same time. Their mouths opened. Then they began chanting, now in unison, now singly, now two of them together. There was no melody and little variation of pitch. Their voices, shrilly nasal, were all so like each other that, if I had shut my eyes, I could not possibly have said at any given moment who was chanting and who was silent. From time to time they paused, paused sometimes for seconds, sometimes for a minute or more than a minute. When they resumed, without a glance at each other, without a prompt from one of their number or anyone else, it was always, as before, in perfect unison, never faltering, never ragged. How did they manage it? Were they all counting to themselves between each lapse into silence and each burst into sound? There was something eerie about it all, as there had been about that dog hurling himself to death on the bonnet of the car.

We must have remained in the church for more than an hour; and all the time, tirelessly, the children went on with their monotonous chanting and all the time the huge congregation – there were people crowded together standing at the back and the sides, and, beyond the wide-flung doors, there were people out in the square – remained totally silent and motionless despite the discomfort and heat. For a while I had thought, in panic, *I can't take this, I've got to get out*, but then, like everyone else, I had suddenly felt composed by the composure of the children, just as previously, in the small, airless room, I had been agitated by the agitation of their relatives.

Out in the square, I drew a deep breath of the rain-impregnated air. Night was now falling over the surrounding mountains. They soared up around the village, jet shading near their summits into a deep violet. Surrounded by people, innumerable silent people, I looked around for Eneas, only to realise that he in turn was looking around for me. I waved. He then began to fight through the crowd to join me.

His face was markedly pale, as he approached me. Then he did an extraordinary thing. He put out his hand and took my hand in his, like a frightened child taking the hand of an adult for refuge or comfort. He continued to hold my hand as we followed the crowd out of the square. He only let go of it when, in order to mount some steps with people pushing us on every side, we had to go one before the other and he then stepped forward first. Far ahead of us, up the pathway which wound up into the mountain behind the church, I could make out the three children marching abreast, with Father Antonio and Diego just behind them. Still, everyone was silent. At my age I soon become puffed when obliged to make a steep ascent, but miraculously I now strode out as I would have done when young.

Eneas peered round at me. 'You are okay?'

[134]

'Fine. Fine.'

Up and up the long procession wound. Then in the darkness ahead of us I heard what sounded like the engine of a car. How had it got up a path so narrow? Perhaps there was also a road.

In fact, the sound came from a generator. A greenish-yellow glare from two arc-lamps was focused on the gaping wound of the cave. Where its entrance soared to a jagged peak, a huge cross had been daubed above it in white paint. Another huge cross had been similarly daubed on a low cushion of rock by the entrance. With remarkable agility for one so old and frail, Father Antonio leapt unaided on to this cushion, his face, in the garish light, looking like a cardboard mask into which the two sunken eyes had been burned. At the base of the rock, looking up at him, the children stood clustered together. He raised both hands. The girlish voice had an extraordinary penetration. Though far back in the crowd, I could nonetheless hear it. What was he saying? I turned to Eneas, hoping for a translation. But he was concentrating too much on the priest, his lower lip drawn in between his teeth and his forehead crumpled in a frown, to notice me. Where was Diego? He was lost somewhere in the crowd.

At what seemed to be an order from Father Antonio, the crowd now began to move back on all sides. I had to move too, under an inexorable pressure, until at my shoulders I felt the hardness of rock. But, trapped like this, innumerable people before me and immovable rock behind me, I felt none of my usual claustrophobia. A flat space, like a small oval arena, had been cleared in the middle, with the now hushed, waiting, spectators ringing it round.

Father Antonio gazed at the children, not imperiously

[135]

but in a hesitant, interrogative manner, one hand half raised and the other resting on his chin. Then, once again as though at some hidden signal, they all simultaneously turned away from him and, led by the boy, filed into the arena. For several seconds they stood there motionless and silent, one behind the other. The crowd was also motionless and silent. Then, at precisely the same moment, they raised their arms, as children do when pretending to be aeroplanes or birds; and, as they did so, they each emitted, in concert, a weird, high-pitched warbling. It was immediately after that they began their running.

I had never before seen anyone, adult or child, run like that. Their bodies arched and their heads thrown backwards, in a manner which would normally be possible only for a contortionist, they began to move not forward but back. At first they moved slowly, from time to time even stumbling, as though this were the first time that they were attempting anything so difficult and strange, and had to get the hang of it. Their pace accelerated; their progress grew surer. Now they were cantering, the boy in the lead, the two girls behind him, effortlessly, their feet rising and falling like pistons thrusting in perfect time with each other. Their back-tilted faces, the eyes unblinking, were paper-white and paper-smooth in the glare from the arc-lamps. Faster and faster they ran, round and round in circles, with the crowd watching them in total absorption. Suddenly, I experienced what I can only describe as awe. It was, I am convinced, what everyone there was experiencing.

As though at another secret signal, all three children slackened their gallop, once again cantered, at last came to a halt. They let their hands fall to their sides. They stared at the entrance to the cave. They showed no sign of effort, no breathlessness, no sweating. Then, as though at yet another secret signal, they walked, the boy once more in the lead and the two girls behind him, towards the cave. The crowd at last broke ranks and surged in behind.

Diego had suddenly appeared beside me. The usually blurred features seemed to have acquired a focus as he put out a hand and gripped my arm: 'You saw! You saw!'

Bemused now, I nodded.

'Have you ever seen anything like that? Have you ever heard of anything like that?'

'No, never.'

'One would have thought that it was impossible to run like that at that speed. And no one in the village has ever seen them practising. I asked Father Antonio that and he said no one, no one.' He broke off, nudged me, pointed ahead.

Standing on tiptoe, I could see the rough stone altar, with steps curving up to it on either side. Above this altar there had been carved a crude representation of the Virgin, the face and hands of which had been daubed with garish paint, so that they stood out harshly, white hands, pink face, vermilion lips, yellow hair, against the greyness of the stone.

I craned my neck upward. The cave soared high above me, in jagged ranges of basalt, one above the other, one behind the other. Was that far-off glimmer the sky? Or was it merely a distant reflection of the arc-light in some vein of quartz?

Suddenly, with a piercing shriek, the boy bounded on to the dolmen of the altar, stretching out his skinny arms to the garish image of the Virgin above it. Heads uptilted, the girls, Father Antonio, Diego, Eneas and I, everyone watched him. Then, as when our party had emerged from the house into the square before making our way through the thickly clotted multitude to the church, that strange shushing and sighing sound, as of some invisible tide sweeping in and then sweeping out again, came from the people all around. Perhaps my own gasp was of wonder and, yes, fear was part of it.

The boy had leapt from the altar, arms outstretched, on to the top of a rock, so far above him that it astounded me that someone so small and so frail-looking should have been able to do so. He perched there, a motionless bird, his eyes unwinking, for a while. Everyone waited. Then, his arms outspread once more as though they were wings, and again emitting that shriek, he seemed not so much to leap as to soar upwards to another, far higher pinnacle of rock. It really seemed that he was flying. From that pinnacle he was suddenly transported, in a diagonal trajectory, to another. And so to another, even higher, even more distant. Each time, just before he made the transition, he let out that shriek, as of someone in agony. Up and up he moved, the spectators' heads now all uptilted to watch him. Meanwhile, before the altar – for a moment I glanced there – the two girls stood patiently waiting. Unlike everyone else, they showed no amazement, indeed showed no emotion whatever. They might have been waiting for the boy to return from some trivial errand.

Now he was fluttering downward, barely touching one jutting rock before brushing past another and another. The rocks were often sharp, his feet were bare. Yet he suffered no injury; and even more amazingly there was none of the expected slap as soft bare soles landed on hard basalt.

Now he had arrived on the altar, alighting once more soundlessly there from a prodigious height of – what? – five or six metres. In the brilliant light now focused on him, his African face was not merely blank, the eyes staring out over the heads of the onlookers, but totally devoid of any sweat, indeed any indication of effort at all. Similarly, there was no sweat on his body, his chest did not heave with a struggle for breath.

Now the two girls clambered on to the altar beside him. They stood on either side of him, hands once more clasped, as his were, behind their backs. I could see, in profile, the lips of the girl nearest to me begin to move. They were all talking, in a low, conversational tone of voice, their heads tilted up to the statue of the Virgin above them. Was this Spanish? Some dialect? No, it could not be either. It was gibberish, I decided. But later Diego was to insist that they must have been talking in Aramaic, and Father Antonio had agreed with him, nodding his head vigorously, when asked for confirmation.

Their voices, always in unison, ran on and on, like some stream flowing slowly but irresistibly between low banks. Then suddenly the voices flowed faster, became tumultuous. The tranquil stream was now a river in flood. The frenzied jabbering was so loud that one might have thought that it was being amplified. My ears began actually to ache with it. Then abruptly it stopped. The children were motionless, staring up at the Virgin. Everyone was motionless, also staring up at Her.

A woman screamed, raising an arm and pointing. Then everyone was screaming, shouting, gasping. Innumerable arms rose, pointed. 'Sí, sí! Sí! Moverse! Moverse!' Did the statue really move? At the time, with a mixture of amazement and, once again, fear, I was sure that it did.

[139]

The head turned slightly, from one side to the other and back again, the lips parted, the right hand rose in acknowledgement and then slowly fell.

'*De nuevo! De nuevo!*' Everyone now seemed to be shouting, everyone now seemed to be imploring a repetition of the miracle. But the statue did not move again. As though nothing had happened, first the boy and then the two girls scrambled off the altar. They might have just decided that it was time to end some game and make for home. One of the girls turned to the boy and said something to him. He put a hand to his simian face and giggled behind it. Then, with a laugh from the other girl, they scampered out through the crowd into the night.

For a while, everyone else remained in the cave. Suddenly I was aware of the strong smell of bodies and, even stronger, of the smell of wet clothes. People had begun to talk, at first in whispers, then more and more loudly, until a babel of voices reverberated up and up in the cave. I felt a hand gripping my forearm. It was Eneas. In the glare from the arc-light his face looked white, smooth, shiny, hard. It might have been made of plastic. There was a look of extraordinary exaltation on it. There was the same look on many of the faces about me.

'*Una revelación!*' It was odd that Eneas should address me in Spanish. '*Increíble.*' Suddenly he threw his arms around me and embraced me. Then he was laughing, laughing uncontrollably, in sheer joy.

That same joy was now sweeping through the crowd, igniting first those nearest to us and then spreading, as though fanned by a hurricane, to those in the farthest corners of the huge cave. Even Father Antonio was laughing, even Diego beside him. Just as Eneas had embraced me, so now many people were embracing each other, as though everyone had suddenly been delivered

[140]

from long imprisonment, a shipwreck, a sentence of death.

I never saw the children again. 'Where have they gone?' I asked as we emerged from the cave, to be told by Father Antonio, through the medium of Diego, that they had gone back to their homes, they must be tired, after all they were only children.

It was at that moment that I heard the sirens and saw the lights bouncing off now one tree and now another in the valley below. The whole crowd halted. A disquietened murmur shivered through them. Someone near me, an old man, said '*Policía?*' on a note of quavering interrogation and then another, stronger voice yelled '*Policía!*' At that there was a babel of cries, some angry, some apprehensive, and everyone began to run in all directions, down the narrow path, into the trees on either side, one or two even back into the cave, no doubt hoping to hide somewhere deep in its recesses. Eneas tugged at my hand. 'Run!' But I remained motionless. Eneas tugged again. Then, with Diego, he sprinted off into the trees.

About a dozen people, Father Antonio and I among them, now remained in front of the cave. We stood there motionless, saying nothing to each other. In my case, perhaps in theirs, a weird kind of paralysis of the will prevented any action. The growl of the cars on the road below grew louder and louder. Father Antonio's lips began to move but no sound emerged. I realised that he was praying.

Now, with guttural shouts and the flashing of torches, men were scrambling up the steep, wooded bank which separated the entrance to the cave from the road below it. '*Alto! guardia!*' But nobody had any impulse to move.

A torch was shone in my face and something was

[141]

shouted at me in Spanish. I replied in English: 'Sorry. I have no idea what you're saying to me.' Later I was to think how absurd that was. The torch moved over my body. Then, amazingly, the dark shape before me – in the glare of the torch I could not see his face – shouted '*Marcha!*' and then in English 'Go, go!'

I stumbled off into the darkness. Why did I not wait to see what happened to Father Antonio? To the others? I was never to be sure of the answer. Forever afterwards I was to feel ashamed of, yes, my cowardice. But, in deserting them, I was only doing to these strangers what Eneas had done to me, a friend.

Somehow I found my way back, in darkness, to the square. It was now totally deserted apart from a mangy dog, sniffing at what looked like a soiled bandage in a gutter. I walked over to Father Antonio's little house, which appeared to be totally in darkness, and knocked on the door. The terrified face of the girl with the hare-lip appeared around it. In a frantic gabble she was asking me something, presumably for news of Father Antonio. I did not know if she had also been at the cave, I supposed that she had. I could merely shrug.

I sat alone in the darkness of the little room. Then I heard voices and rushed out into the hall. Eneas and Diego were there. The two of them seemed to be arguing.

When Diego saw me, he said: 'I'm telling Eneas that he must hide until the police have gone. It doesn't matter for you and me to be here, but for him it could be disastrous.' His voice was agitated.

'Yes, Eneas, I think Diego's right.'

Eneas shook his head. 'There is Father Antonio. Perhaps I can do something for Father Antonio. As a policeman I may be able to persuade them . . .'

'You'll only make things worse,' Diego said.

For a while the two men argued in Spanish until, repeatedly pushing him towards the door, Diego at last got Eneas to leave the house.

Diego and I sat down, each on a straightbacked, wooden chair, facing each other.

'Is there any of that rum left?' he asked after a short while.

'Yes, in the boot of the car.' He looked puzzled by the word 'boot'. 'The trunk,' I said. 'I left it unlocked.'

Without asking if he could have any, Diego rose with a sigh and quitted the room. When he returned, the bottle was at his lips and he was gulping at it. He held it out to me. I shook my head. He gulped again. Replacing the cork and then wiping the back of his hand across his mouth, he said: 'Now I feel better.'

'Good.'

He sat down, the bottle beside him, leaned forward in the chair, clasped his hands between his knees. For someone so large those hands, I suddenly noticed, were strangely small and delicate. If one had seen them by themselves, one would have guessed them to be the hands of a woman.

'I knew they would come. They had to come. The only surprise is that they did not come sooner.'

I wanted to ask why, if he had known that the police would come, he had not persuaded Eneas to stay away. Instead I asked: 'Do you think that Eneas will be all right?'

He shrugged. 'I hope they will not find him. But Cuba is full of informers. That is one of the most terrible things about a government like ours. Your friends inform on you, not only your enemies. And perhaps – if you need

[143]

something enough or you want something enough or you are frightened enough – you, in turn, inform on your friends.'

'I'm glad I've never had that experience.'

Diego gave a bitter smile. 'You have many things for which to be glad.' From the tone, an outsider might have supposed that he despised and disliked me. Perhaps he really did.

There was a long silence. Again he gulped from the bottle.

'So . . . what do you think?'

'What do I think about what?'

'About what we saw, about what we heard. A miracle?' He leaned towards me. I could smell the rum on his breath and the stale sweat on his massive body. 'Was it a miracle? What do you think?'

'I don't know what to think. I don't believe in miracles. But . . .' I shrugged. 'Did that boy really fly? Or was it a hallucination, a mass hallucination? And the Virgin – did she really move?' Later, much later, after I had gone back to England, I had remembered that warm water tinged with an orange sheen, its bitter taste lingering for a long, long time on my tongue. Was it possible that some chemical seeped into the spring and that that chemical could induce hallucinations, just as ergot had done in the Middle Ages, when miracles not dissimilar were constantly reported? Perhaps the extraordinary energy of the boy, leaping from rock to rock, now vertically, now horizontally, was the result of some such chemical derangement of the nervous system.

'What do you think?'

With total certainty he replied: 'I think that we were present at a miracle. For me, it's not the first time. Once

[144]

in the leper colony ... a woman ...' His voice trailed away, as though he had suddenly remembered something which he had thought to have forgotten forever.

'Yes?'

'A cure. A total cure.' He smiled. 'But of course some of my colleagues had their rational explanations. As no doubt you will eventually have a rational explanation of everything that took place tonight.'

I started at the sound of a car drawing up outside the house, followed by raised voices. Diego went to the window, raised the curtain, peered out.

'He's returned.'

'Eneas?'

But it was Father Antonio, brought back by the police in one of their cars. Three officers lumbered into the room, with Father Antonio between the middle-aged man in front – a captain, I assumed – and the two young men behind.

The captain pointed at me and said: '*El extranjero?*' I wondered if this was the same man who had shone the torch on me outside the cave and had then told me to beat it.

In Spanish Diego began to explain that I was from England, a tourist, who had heard a report of what had been happening at the village and had then wanted to investigate.

The captain grinned at me, in no way malevolent or even disapproving. Then he turned to Father Antonio and said something. Father Antonio nodded, then looked at me and shrugged and smiled, hands outspread, as though in apology. The Cubans all then left the room.

I sat on alone. Then, more because I was bored than because I felt any need for it, I picked up the bottle of rum and took a gulp. The idea of Diego's lips resting where my lips were now resting filled me with disgust. But I gulped again and yet again.

Eventually the five Cubans returned. Diego stooped for the rum bottle and held it out to the captain. To my amazement the captain took it and drank. The back of his hand brushing the moustache which cascaded over his upper lip, he said: *'Gracias.'* He smiled. It was difficult to believe that any harm could come to anyone from someone so friendly and relaxed.

Father Antonio and Diego returned from seeing the men out. I could hear the police-car starting up with a series of coughs and then grinding off.

'What a shit!'

I was surprised and dismayed. 'Is there going to be trouble?'

'Of course. He'll make his report and then – in a week or a month – the trouble will start.'

'Trouble for him?' I indicated Father Antonio, who had collapsed on to a chair, his chin on his chest, his eyes closed, in meditation, in exhaustion or in sleep, it was impossible to say which.

'Of course. But also for everyone in the village. And for the children. Especially for the children.'

I was appalled. 'For the children?'

'Yes. Of course.' Diego then began to tell me what was the message given to them by the Virgin. In October of that same year El Commandante would die, would die by an act of violence. Then everything would change, everything would be better. The Virgin had promised that. The Virgin would never break her promise.

'How many people know what the Virgin is supposed to have told the children?' A vestige of scepticism made me insert that 'is supposed to have'.

[146]

'First a few people in the village knew. Then everyone in the village. Then people in the surrounding villages. Then more and more people in Havana and Santiago and Trinidad. Such secrets are never easy to keep. And when people are living in despair . . .'

'Why didn't you or Eneas tell me before?'

Diego did not answer.

'Didn't you trust me?'

Again Diego did not answer.

After that conversation, the two of us waited on and on in silence for Eneas to return. Eventually, venturing out into the now deserted square, Diego established that the police had all gone. In small groups the former spectators were returning. Some reported that they had been rounded up by the police and obliged to show their identity cards. Others had been successful in concealing themselves. By now I too was out in the square, with Diego. 'Many of these people will now walk home. Many miles. A few will bicycle. A very few will go by car or truck.' One such group was clambering aboard their truck in total silence. Another truck rattled past, vomiting a foul-smelling smoke.

Suddenly Eneas appeared from behind the church. With him were two young girls, plump, almost stout, with round faces and thick black hair falling in ringlets to their shoulders. They could have been sisters. As he approached, his pace was slow, with frequent interruptions when he stopped in his tracks to face them to tell them something. From time to time I heard his robust laughter or the tinkle of theirs. All the extraordinary events of that evening might never have happened. I felt a sudden rage.

As he neared us, Eneas gave a wave. Then he told me: 'I met these two young ladies hiding in that barn over

[147]

there.' He pointed up the hillside. 'I went there also to hide. I was fortunate, yes?'

'Very fortunate.' I could not keep my resentment out of my voice.

Either Eneas was unaware of that resentment or he decided to ignore it.

'They have gone?'

'Yes, they've gone,' Diego confirmed. 'But I was saying to our English friend that they'll certainly come back. I hope there's not going to be any trouble for you.'

'They did not see me.'

Diego shrugged. 'Other people saw you.'

'No one who knows me.'

The girls began to excuse themselves in Spanish. Eneas put a hand on the bare arm of the one closest to him and said something. He must have been urging her to stay. Both the girls giggled. Then their giggling became laughter, as they covered their crimsoning faces with their hands.

Diego chuckled. 'That is not a nice thing to say to two innocent girls,' he said.

'These two are not innocent,' Eneas countered.

'Of course they are!'

Eneas laughed. 'You were not in the barn with us!'

Eventually, with many backward looks, the girls sauntered off, arm in arm.

'*Guapas!*' Eneas called out after them. Their responding laughter echoed round the square.

'So what do we do now?' Diego asked. 'Do we drive back to Havana in the dark?'

In the end, as the three of us drank syrupy cups of tea with him in the small, stuffy room, Father Antonio persuaded us to stay. What had the police said to him? Diego asked. Then, constantly turning to me, he translated the priest's answer for me. The old man was clearly so exhausted that the words kept stumbling and collapsing. Oh, they had been polite, they had done him no harm. But . . . well, there would certainly be trouble. This was a time when the government was fearful of what might happen; and when people were afraid, they were apt to do terrible things. But he didn't care. He was too old now to care. They could do with him what they wished. To die at home or to die in prison – it made little difference.

Eventually, with Eneas's assistance, the old man staggered to his feet. He would show us our room, he said. He slept here – he pointed at a closed door – and here – he opened another door – was the room that we could have. Usually his housekeeper and her daughter slept in it but the housekeeper's sister was ill and they had gone to her house to spend the night with her.

Father Antonio having disappeared into his room, the three of us went into ours. The window had been boarded up, presumably because the pane had been broken and it had either been impossible or too expensive to replace it. There was little air, and there was a sour smell as of vomit. A huge bed, covered with a long, hard bolster and a blanket far too narrow, took up at least three quarters of the space. The rest of the space was taken up by a breakfront mahogany wardrobe, an oddly high table, put together from what looked like unseasoned wood, and two chairs. From the back of one of these chairs some black, much-darned women's stockings dangled.

I looked in dismay at the bed. 'Are we all three expected to sleep in that?'

'In Cuba not everyone enjoys the luxury of a bed to himself.' It was Diego's old needling tone.

[149]

'Perhaps it would be better if we drove back to Havana.'

'I'm too tired,' Diego said firmly. 'Eneas has no licence. Have you got a licence?'

I said that I had. Then I thought of driving, in the dark and in a state of exhaustion, over those rough roads, little more than tracks. 'But I don't feel I can . . .'

'Then we stay here,' Diego said. He gave an abrupt laugh. 'I'll sleep in the car. That'll give you both more room.'

At first I was taken aback. Then, like water suddenly rushing into a cistern, excitement began to fill me.

'Will that be all right for you?'

'Well, it won't be comfortable. But it'll be more comfortable than sleeping on that bed with two snoring people.'

'I don't snore.'

'That's what snorers always say.'

Ostensibly we were joking with each other; but there was a rasping undertow of bitterness.

Suddenly Eneas announced: 'I am hungry.'

'Well, there are still some tins in the car. And some bread – though by now that'll be pretty dry, I should think.'

'In Cuba we are used to dry bread – if there's any bread at all,' Diego put in.

Even while I was getting the food out of the boot, Diego was clambering into the back of the Lada. When I peered in, he was lying on his side, his knees drawn up, a hand under his chin.

'You look terribly uncomfortable.'

'It is terribly uncomfortable. But never mind. It would, as I said, be even more uncomfortable on that bed.'

'Would you like some food?'

'No, thank you.'

'Well – in that case – sleep well!'

'The same to you,' he murmured, twisting his body away from me, as though even now the discomfort was becoming intolerable. Perhaps it was. He was, after all, a large man, and the car was a tiny one.

Back in the little room, Eneas drew the penknife out of his pocket preparatory to opening the tin of Spam. 'You don't need to use that,' I told him. Then I demonstrated how to use the key. '*Maravilloso!*' he exclaimed in wonderment.

He held the opened tin out to me. I shook my head. 'I'm too tired to feel hungry.' With one of the plastic spoons, he began to wolf down the contents. Once he paused to look up and beam.

'All right?' I asked.

'Terrific!' That day he had heard me use the word and had repeated it after me, as he so often did when he heard a word or phrase new to him. He was an eager and quick learner.

Now I went off to the lavatory, down the corridor, which I had used earlier in the day. No more than a hole in the ground, with two worn-away rests for the feet, it demanded a gymnastic ability which, at my age, I no longer possess. On my previous visit I had all but toppled in, while lowering myself. This time it was merely necessary for me to stand astride. There was an oblong slate sink with a tap above it. Water trickled out when I turned the tap, and I splashed it over my face. My chin and upper lip felt rough. I would not be able to shave the next morning. I could not brush my teeth now. Fifty, even forty years ago, such things would not have bothered me.

As though he had been too fatigued to dispose of them,

[151]

Eneas had left the empty tin and the open penknife on the chair on which he had been sitting. Over its back, presumably covering the woman's stockings, he had thrown his jeans and his tee-shirt. Underneath it were the shoes which I had bought for him. He himself was already on the bed, his face to the wall, knees drawn up and the thin blanket almost wholly covering him.

I removed my own jacket, trousers, shirt, shoes, placing them tidily – as each night I place my clothes tidily, ever since my prep-school days – on the other chair. Then I clambered on to the bed. Hell – the light! There was no bedside one. I got off the bed again and crossed over to the switch. As I reached it, Eneas stirred, groaned, then sat up.

'What time is it?'

He must have imagined that he had been sleeping a long time.

I laughed. 'You can't have been on that bed for more than ten minutes.'

Eneas also now laughed, with the same joy with which he had laughed in the cave. 'What an evening! It was true, it was all true!'

'What was true?' I had now moved over to the bed, to sit on its edge beside him.

'In Cuba one is always hearing of these miracles – which are not miracles. People wish to believe and so – they believe!' Again he gave that joyous laugh. 'But you saw! And you are not a Cuban, you have no reason to believe only because you wish to believe. You saw, yes?'

I nodded. I did not wish to destroy his exultant mood by voicing any doubts. 'Yes, it was extraordinary. I think the most extraordinary thing I've ever seen. Such things just don't happen in the world which I've known for

[152]

almost seventy years. And yet – they did happen, they did!'

'At last we have hope. In October – the death of Fidel ... I believe that it will happen, I truly believe. If all the other things happened, then that will happen too. Oh, I am so happy, I am so happy!'

Once again I was conscious of something unformed, something childishly malleable in his character. At one moment he was flirting with two peasant girls as if all the amazing events of the evening had never taken place. Now those same events had filled him with this exaltation.

'Come!' he held out his arms. 'It is time for us sleep.'

I went over and switched out the light; then by the glimmer from the small, high window, I made my way back to the bed.

At first I lay near to its edge, careful that my body should nowhere make the contact which I was longing to make. It was as though a wayfarer, parched with thirst, perversely refused to approach near enough to drink from the spring on which he had stumbled. But lying there, my eyes open, I seemed to hear each of Eneas's heart-beats as if he were pressed close to me.

Suddenly – was he still awake? – he shifted with what sounded like half a sigh and half an exclamation of annoyance, and his left leg was against my right one. I did not move, I did not dare to move. Seconds passed. Then he turned over and his arm was across me, the hand resting on my shoulder. The hand moved, it grasped the shoulder, kneaded it, kneaded it with such violence that, the next day, the flesh was discoloured. Then he jerked me over to him.

Until that moment I had initiated nothing. Now, with

[153]

a groan, I clutched at him and pressed my lips against his. But, clamping his mouth shut, he refused me anything but the rigid barrier of his teeth. When I made another attempt to insert my tongue, he jerked his head away, with a muffled 'No, no!'

Fearfully I lowered my hand, to touch first his flat belly, then one of his thighs, then eventually his cock. Amazingly, miraculously, I met with no resistance. I could feel his breath coming in short gasps against my cheek. He gave a groan. His cock, now erect, began to throb in my hand.

In comparison with innumerable other nights spent with innumerable other people in the course of a promiscuous and much-travelled life, I found the love-making which followed abrupt, hurried, clumsy, crude. And yet, with total truthfulness, I can say 'That was the best.' To Eneas too I said those words in the immediate aftermath: 'That was the best.' But he had already turned away from me, pulling the blanket off me in order wholly to cover that magnificent body of his. I lay in the dark. I felt an extraordinary energy and a happiness no less extraordinary. '*Milagro*,' Diego had said of what had happened with the children. This was another miracle, smaller yes, but a miracle nonetheless. It was as though a withered branch had suddenly put forth flowers.

How could I sleep, how could I possibly sleep?

But eventually I did sleep, deeply, dreamlessly, unaware of that body close to mine, unaware of the mosquitoes whose raging bites drove me to a frenzy of scratching throughout the next day, unaware of the usual demands of my bladder and of Father Antonio attending more than once (as he confessed, in apology for any possible noise, the next day) to the demands of his.

When I awoke, early the next morning, I still felt that

[154]

extraordinary energy and that extraordinary happiness – the miracle renewed. Eneas was still sleeping, on his back now, the blanket almost entirely off him. One hand, the fingers slightly curled, was resting on his forehead. His cheeks and neck were flushed. For a long time I stared at him, my body propped up on an elbow. Then I gave the blanket a small tug, so that none of it now covered him. He was wearing old-fashioned boxer shorts, darned here and there, presumably by either his dead mother or his grandmother, and yellow from frequent washing. He had a huge erection.

I put out a hand, hesitated, then rested it on his thigh. I began to stroke the warm flesh. Eneas gave a little murmur, shifted his body a fraction. I moved the hand, slowly, gently.

Suddenly, with an inarticulate shout – it was as though a gun had suddenly been fired just behind my head – he leapt off the bed. 'What are you doing? No! *No!*'

I put a finger to my lips. I frowned, shook my head. What if Father Antonio were to hear? My heart was racing with terror.

'What are you? What are you?' he demanded.

Then he stooped, picked the still open penknife off the chair and hurled it at me.

It struck me on the cheek and clattered to the floor. I put up a hand. Strangely, despite the ferocity of the impact, I then felt no pain. But there was something warm and moist on my palm. Blood.

Eneas was staring in horror at me. 'What have you made me do? *Idiota!*'

I stared back. I felt a hysterical impulse to laugh. 'What have you made *me* do?' I asked.

He fumbled in the pockets of his jeans and produced a crumpled, far from clean handkerchief. He held it out.

[155]

When, my hand still to my cheek, which was now not oozing but trickling blood, I did not take it from him, he strode over and, with an exclamation of annoyance, pressed it to the wound. Our two bodies were rigid, totally separate.

There was a knock on the door. It was Diego. 'Are you awake?' he called out. When there was no answer, the knock was repeated and he called out even louder 'Are you awake?' The door opened. 'We ought to make an early start. Before the day gets too hot.' He stared at us both. 'What's happened?' But even then I felt that there had been no need for him to ask that question. Somehow he had all along known what would happen, and now he knew what had happened.

'He fell,' Eneas said, still pressing the handkerchief to my cheek. He went on talking to Diego, now in Spanish. Having begun to feel faintly sick and giddy, I made no attempt to understand what it was that they were saying.

Father Antonio shuffled in. Soon, having been told of the accident, he shuffled off again, to return with a bottle of iodine. I protested – it wasn't necessary, the wound wasn't deep – but he insisted on dabbing on the iodine with a wad of coarse lavatory paper. I drew in my breath sharply as I felt the sting. Diego laughed. He seemed to be enjoying my discomfiture.

Throughout the long drive back – the car seemed even hotter, the road even rougher – Eneas hardly spoke to me. When I offered him food, he muttered *'Gracias'* (it was significant that he now used Spanish) and when he accidentally kicked me while clambering out of the car for some mineral water, he similarly muttered *'Lo siento.'* But that was all.

[156]

Diego, on the other hand, chattered away, telling me about his experiences in Africa, about a visit which he had once paid to Oxford for a conference, about the English and American writers whom he admired (rarely ones which I admired) and about the films which he had recently seen. I was feeling desolate. I was feeling exhausted. I wished that he would shut up.

By the time that we drew up outside the hotel, it was already late afternoon.

'Would you like to come in for a drink or something to eat?'

Eneas said nothing. It was Diego who answered: 'Thank you, but I have some things I must do.'

'Shall I see you later today?' Now I addressed Eneas alone.

At first I thought that I was going to get no answer at all. Then, in the sulky voice of a disappointed child, he said: 'Not today. Sorry. I too have some things I must do.'

'Tomorrow morning then?'

'How can I see you tomorrow morning?' Suddenly he sounded not sulky but angry. 'Tomorrow I must work.'

'Tomorrow! But I thought you said . . .'

He shook his head. 'Tomorrow I must work. I told you!'

He had told me nothing of the kind. But it was useless to argue. 'Well, what about tomorrow evening?'

He shrugged.

'Okay?'

To my relief, he mumbled 'Okay.'

Head averted, he hung around while Diego and I said our goodbyes. Then, with dragging footsteps, he began to move off.

'Goodbye, Eneas! See you tomorrow evening!'

He did not answer.

Diego looked at me, raised his shoulders, smiled. That smile, I convinced myself, expressed only one thing: derisive satisfaction.

# 16

Without Eneas's company, I was at a loss how to pass the day. For a while I read in my bedroom; but then the little maid appeared with her plastic bucket containing her cleaning things, and I got up and left her to her work.

My attempts to read in the pocket-handkerchief of a park met with even less success. Constantly I was badgered either by touts or by people who merely wanted to talk to me for lack of anything better to do. Some of the latter were attractive young men and, in two cases, attractive older men. But whereas I would normally have been happy to chat to them, now I had no inclination to do so. My answers to their questions were perfunctory, I put no questions to them myself. When one of them asked me the time, I said that I did not know, even though the man must have seen the watch on my wrist; and when one of them begged for a cigarette, I said that I had none, even though he might well have seen me puffing at one only a short time before. I could not even be interested when two women, prostitutes I assumed, began to scream at each other, just in front of where I was sitting, and eventually began to fight, clutching each other's hair and malevolently kicking. It was left to a passing taxi-driver to separate them. All three then began to laugh, the women patting their elaborate coiffures into place and brushing down their clothes while they did so.

Eventually I got up and once more wandered through the Museo Nacional de Bellas Artes. But nothing now made any impression on me. I was consumed both with a desire to see Eneas again and with the dread that I had totally destroyed our relationship.

I was wandering through the streets of old Havana, depressed, as I had hardly been depressed in the past, by the filth, the noise, the emaciated dogs, the crumbling, murky tenements which had once been palaces, when I thought: 'Raul lives near here.' I had so often told myself 'Well, that's someone I certainly don't wish to see again.' But now I turned down one street and looked for another one, and then consulted my map.

Once again the dogs set up their yapping; and once again the unshaven face, the eyes bleary with sleep and drink, appeared round the door. But this time, instead of the grumpy instruction to come back another time, Raul was welcoming.

'*Amigo!* Where have you been? Why have you not come to see me?'

I tried to excuse myself as Raul repeated the question when we had sat down: I had been so much taken up with my sightseeing, there had been other introductions, my friend at the Embassy had tended to monopolise me. A glass in his hand – again he had offered me nothing – Raul looked over at me quizzically. I did not think that he believed me. As so often in such circumstances, I was making the mistake of producing far too many excuses.

'Did you like Cesaro?'

'Oh, yes, yes, Thank you so much for sending him along. He's . . . very nice. And very attractive.'

[160]

'Didn't you wish to see him again?'

'Well, as I told you . . . But perhaps, before I leave . . . Perhaps the two of you could come to dinner with me at La Bodeguita del Medio.'

He gave a scoffing laugh. 'Not La Bodeguita del Medio. The only thing it offers is what the guidebooks call "atmosphere". The food is terrible. You can take us to La Criolla.'

'All right. La Criolla it is.' But I had no intention of taking them anywhere.

'So-o-o . . .' Raul reached out for a crushed packet of cigarettes, drew one out, lit it. 'You have been having many adventures?'

'Not the kind of adventures that I imagine you mean. I'm afraid my days for those are over. But I've been having an interesting time.'

Suddenly I was overmastered by a desire to speak about what had happened in the cave, even though I knew that later I would regret it. 'I had an extraordinary adventure yesterday,' I began.

'Oh, yes?'

'I had this introduction to a priest,' I lied. 'A priest who spent many years in Africa. And he told me about some strange things that had been happening in the mountains beyond Pinar del Rio.'

Raul drew deeply on the pinched fragment of cigarette between his nicotine-stained fingers. Then he ground it out in a used cup lying on its side in a litter of papers on the table before him. 'I think that I know what you are going to tell me.'

'You've heard about it?'

He nodded. 'I wanted to go there myself. But without a car, without any buses . . . If you had told me you were going, I could have gone with you.' He stared fixedly at

[161]

me in accusation. Then he said, reaching out for yet another cigarette: 'So what did you see, what did you hear?'

I began to tell him; but in telling him, I once again omitted any mention of Eneas. Raul listened in silence, without any interruption, his bleary, red-rimmed eyes under their bushily untidy eyebrows fixed not on my eyes but on my mouth.

When I had finished the story, he sighed, leaned forward, pulled out the stained cushion behind him. Resting it on his knees, he punched it repeatedly, and with each punch, he exclaimed: 'Good! Good! Good!' Then he said: 'Do you have any doubts? . . . Do you?' He leaned forward again, searching my face.

'I've told you what I saw, what I heard. But for someone like myself, someone who has never had any religious belief, someone sceptical, rational . . .' I broke off.

He shook his head, a knowing adult to an innocent child. 'It will happen,' he said. He lowered his voice, even though there was no possibility that anyone could overhear us. 'El Commandante will die.' He burst into throaty laughter, which then became a cough. Thumping on his chest as he had previously thumped on the cushion, he got out: 'Or, if he doesn't die – if the Virgin has fooled us – he'll have to run away. He has his estate in Spain, the King has told him he can live there whenever he wishes. And he has his ranch in Argentina. And other properties. He will die or he will go. That's certain.'

'I hope you're right.'

'Of course I'm right. Hasn't Our Lady promised it?'

I did not know whether the question was put seriously or in jest.

At the door, when I was leaving, he put a hand on my

shoulder: 'Oh, *amigo*, one thing. When you next come to see me – and I hope you will come to see me – be a good boy and bring me a bottle of gin. Will you do that? Yes? Beefeater, that's the gin I like. But Gordon's will do, Gordon's is easier to find in Cuba.'

I said that I would try to find some Beefeater.

That evening I sat in the foyer, waiting for Eneas. What a fool I had been not to ask him what time he would come! I had just assumed that it would be the usual time.

Tel passed, with the tall woman with whom I had seen him before. 'We're off to the ballet!' he announced. Then, looking back over his shoulder as the woman swayed out into the street ahead of him, he pulled a face at me. Clearly the ballet was not his but his companion's choice.

The young man on guard by the door wandered over. For a while he stood near me, arms crossed, staring out through the window, as I myself had been doing. Then he said: 'You wait for your friend?'

'Yes.'

'Late.'

'Yes, late.'

He gave me a rueful smile and wandered off. Once I might have been interested in him, since in his clumsy, peasant way he was far from unattractive. I might have attempted to detain him further by chatting on to him. I might even have suggested a drink when he ceased to be on duty. But now I was totally uninterested.

Nine o'clock came, ten o'clock. Normally I should have finished eating by now, and I had eaten nothing. But I was not hungry; and in any case I had no wish to go into the dining-room, now wholly deserted, with no one to whom to talk except the waiter.

[163]

At eleven o'clock I trudged up to bed. It was clear that Eneas was not coming. Perhaps he would never come? The desolate, terrifying thought suddenly transfixed me. Perhaps this was the end? I felt as I would have felt if a consultant had said to me: 'I'm afraid there's nothing more we can do for you.'

Numb with terror, I began slowly to take off my clothes. Could this be the end, *could* it? Oh, no, Eneas must have been detained at his work. Perhaps some colleague had fallen ill and he had been told to stand in for him. Perhaps there had been some emergency. Perhaps – yes, why not? – there had been a crisis at home.

But he could have telephoned!

Perhaps he *had* telephoned – or had tried to telephone. The system was so faulty that he might never have got through. Or he might have got through only to be told that I had left the hotel or that I was out, or to be put through to Tel or someone like him, just as more than once I myself had had total strangers put through to me.

I sat on the bed. And then, suddenly, agonisingly, I saw that outstretched body, the back of the powerful hand resting, the fingers curled, on the forehead, the nipples prominent on the swelling chest, and the cock lying sideways under those much-darned, yellowing boxer shorts.

I got up and went to the small Florentine leather box in which, for years now, I had kept my medicines when I was travelling. I shook one sleeping-pill out from its bottle and then another. I poured out some mineral water, luke-warm because I had forgotten to replace the bottle in the mini-bar.

I swallowed the pills.

But I could not sleep.

[164]

After two or three hours, I got off the bed and took a cold shower.

Then I sat by the window, *Les Caves du Vatican* lying unread on my knees, and waited for the dawn.

# 17

How was I to get hold of him?

Repeatedly I walked past the police station, peering in through the doors left permanently open because of the heat. On the second occasion that I did so, the young homosexual who had given me that look of sly complicity on the day of the attempted theft was once more there, standing by the dais, hands on hips and mouth pursed, as he gazed out. When he saw me peering in, he raised his thin eyebrows, smiled, then lifted a hand in the briefest of greetings. Was it merely a coincidence that he was once more there? Or could it be that he was an informer or even a plain-clothes detective? In my present distracted, self-blaming mood, I was disturbed by his presence. I even began to suspect, succumbing to paranoia as I so often do when anxious and depressed, that the youth's being there might have something to do with Eneas and myself. But how was that possible?

An hour or two later, when again I was passing, I saw with relief that he had gone. Standing at the desk on the dais was the beautiful woman officer who had been so friendly to me. On an impulse I walked in. As I approached her, she stared at me with a faintly puzzled, faintly startled expression, as though we had never met. Did foreigners so often turn up that she had forgotten who I was?

With what little Spanish I possessed, I asked if Eneas De León were there. She looked at me blankly. I pointed at the door beyond which lay the office in which Eneas and I had first met and repeated my question. She shrugged, then turned away to say something to a short, portly officer who had just swaggered in.

A middle-aged woman who had been sitting reading a book on one of the benches now got up and waddled over. She had a round, nondescript, good-natured face, and was wearing a large straw hat, its elastic band biting deep into a flabby dewlap.

'Can I help?'

'Oh, that's very kind of you. I'm looking for a friend of mine, a friend who works here.'

'What is his name, please?'

I told her.

She turned to the woman officer and began to translate. As she did so, the officer never looked at either her or me, but instead kept her eyes on the battered ledger, its pages grubby and curling, open before her on the desk.

When the woman had finished, the officer looked up. She said a few hurried, indifferent words, then picked up a pen and began to scribble something on a scrap of paper.

'He is not here. He is away. Maybe away for many days.'

'But where is he? Could you please ask her that? *Where is he?*'

'I will try.' Again the officer did not look at the woman. Seated now, she continued to inspect the ledger,

[167]

impatiently flicking over its pages as though in search of something.

Once again the woman translated for me. 'She does not know where he is. He was called away this morning.'

'Called away? But why? How?'

After some more conferring: 'She is sorry, she does not know.' Then, squinting at me through her spectacles, she added ominously: 'Or maybe she does know, but is not allowed to tell you. That is also possible.'

'It seems so strange. I saw him only yesterday. We – we had a rendezvous.'

'*Rendezvous?*'

'A meeting. We had arranged a meeting. He never came.'

The woman pulled a little face, the corners of her wide mouth turning downward and her eyes half closing. Had she understood what I was saying?

'He never came,' I repeated. 'He promised to come. He never came.' The woman was turning away from me, about to move off. I caught her arm. 'Could you ask her – is there any way of getting in touch with him?'

The officer replied, in effect, No, although she took some time to do so. At last she was actually looking at me, with an expression which struck me as a baffling mixture of compassion, disapproval and contempt.

I left the police station and, at a loss where to go next or what to do, entered a bar, recommended in my guidebook, opposite to it. Over a glass of Havana Club 7 in a dingy corner, I gave way to anger and despair. What the hell was going on? Gulping at the rum, I considered all the possibilities. Perhaps, in remorse and shame for his behaviour and in disgust with mine, Eneas had decided that he did not want to see me again. That could have happened. It had happened in the case of one other person, a married builder, who, while working for me, had in effect seduced me and had then failed ever to turn up again, to complete the job or even to be paid. Or it could be that his presence in the cave had somehow been discovered and he was now in trouble. Yes, why not? Perhaps he had been demoted and posted elsewhere. Perhaps he had been summarily dismissed from the service. Perhaps – Christ! – he was in gaol.

Oh, you're being melodramatic, I told myself at that point. What is most likely is that some job came in for which he was thought to be ideally suited. Or that someone fell ill somewhere else and he was regarded as the best person to take over. He had to leave in a hurry and he had no way of letting you know. And the woman officer, clearly a subordinate, has no idea where he has been sent. Why should she?

All at once, in the gloom, I was aware of someone standing by the table. I looked up. Then, with a jolt not merely of surprise but also of alarm, I realised that it was the young homosexual from the police station. He smiled down at me, revealing front teeth which – for the first time I noticed it – had a large gap between them.

'Good morning,' he said, in a soft, ingratiating voice, even though it was already past two.

I made no answer, briefly frowning up at him and then turning my head away.

He drew back the chair opposite to mine, its legs screeching across the bare boards, and nonchalantly seated himself. He crossed an ankle high over a knee, he leaned forward. 'May I talk English with you?', he asked in a low, confidential voice.

'What? ... No, I'm sorry. I have to go back to my hotel.' I looked around for the waiter but could see him nowhere.

[169]

'I walk with you to your hotel.'

'No. No, thank you.'

'I walk with you.'

'No. I want to walk alone. *I want to walk alone.*'

'I can show you good time.'

'Thank you.' I shook my head. 'No.'

He laughed impudently. 'Why you not want good time? I think you like good time. I take you to my house. Good house. Clean.' Again he gave that impudent laugh. He leaned across the table, then put a hand on my forearm. *'Cheap,'* he hissed.

I had seen the waiter. I got up and hurried over to him. He was in conversation with two girls, but I had no compunction in interrupting him. *'La cuenta, por favor!'* The waiter's slowness was, I was sure, deliberate – he wished to punish me for my rudeness; and meanwhile the youth stood waiting at my shoulder, his hands once again on his narrow hips, one foot in its pointed slipper extended ahead of the other, and that unattractive gap in his teeth exposed by a mocking smile.

Out in the glare, the youth took my arm, saying: 'Come, mister. This way. My house not far. Good house. Come, come!'

I pulled myself free. Then, amazing myself, I was suddenly shouting: 'Oh, leave me! Leave me alone! Go away! I don't want to talk to you! I don't want to have anything to do with you. Leave me alone!'

Everyone in the street halted, to gaze at us. A woman gave a titter. A passerby, almost doubled over by the bulging sack on his back, called out a few words. Then all around me laughter exploded and fizzed. The youth was saying something in a loud, contemptuous voice, when a hand from behind me shoved me, shoved me so violently that I stumbled and all but fell over. I turned. It was one of the two prostitutes who had accosted me on my first evening in Havana.

Suddenly I was afraid.

I began to stride away. Behind me a falsetto voice – the youth's or someone else's – screamed *'Maracon!'* Then I heard even louder laughter.

Everyone seemed to be laughing.

I was breathless when I reached my room. I threw myself on my bed, I buried my face in the pillow, I moaned over and over *Oh, Christ, Christ, Christ!*


She was a charming girl, she wanted to help me if she possibly could do so. But, having first offered me a cup of coffee, which I refused, she began to explain the problem. Although I had travelled to Cuba on my own, I had really been part of a package tour.

What package tour?

Well, perhaps I had met that party of English people in my hotel?

Did she mean the communists?

She gave a little smile and brushed a wing of glossy, black hair away from her face. She didn't know whether they were communists or not. They were tourists, English tourists, and they had come to Cuba to see schools and hospitals and agricultural cooperatives, that was all she knew about them. I was part of that tour, I had to go back with that tour. If I hadn't been part of that tour, I'd have had to pay far more for my air ticket.

But couldn't I just return exactly a week later? There must be tours coming out every week, weren't there?

Yes, oh yes, she nodded. More and more English people were visiting Cuba. But the difficulty was that, on the Friday following the one on which I was due to leave, the plane was already fully booked. Not a seat, not a single seat.

'Oh, hell! Then what am I to do? I must, must stay for another week. I can't possibly leave the day after tomorrow.'

'There are other planes. For example, you could take one of the ordinary Air Cubana flights. Or there is Air Iberia. You might even be able to get a Martinair flight to Amsterdam from Varadero. That's really meant to be only for Dutch tourists but there are often empty seats. Very cheap,' she added.

'So you mean I'll have to pay all over again for a ticket to London?'

'I am sorry.' Again she tossed back that wing of hair from her face. 'What can I do?'

What could I myself do? I had spent far more on this holiday than I had ever planned, recklessly charging up meals, drinks and purchases from the hotel shop and the diplomatic shop to one or other of my three credit cards. Back in London my current account was already in the red.

'Well, I suppose I'd better book on the Air Cubana flight.'

'Club class, first class?'

'Good God, no! The cheapest class available.'

At that we both began to laugh.

# 18

For two days I wandered the streets, crazily imagining that round that corner, in that open-air café, in the Coppelia ice-cream park, outside this or that museum, I would suddenly come on Eneas.

*Eneas! What happened to you? Why did you never get in touch?*

*Amigo, amigo! I am so glad! Let me explain. There was this problem – this terrible problem . . . But now it is solved.*

From time to time, I yet again walked up the narrow street in which my bag had been snatched and yet again walked down the even narrower street in which the policeman had towered threateningly over the skinny black culprit and had then hit him across the head so violently that he had all but fallen over. Then, walking slowly past the police station, I yet again peered in. Often the beautiful woman officer was there; but if she noticed me, she gave no sign. Fortunately I never again saw the young homosexual.

Once, as I approached the station, three officers were getting out of a police-car. It was him, it was him! The second of them was him! I rushed towards the car. Then I saw that this man had a puffy face, a small, retroussé nose, thin eyebrows over greenish-yellow eyes. How could I have imagined him to be Eneas? It was his tall, broad-shouldered physique that had brutally deceived me.

Wandering endlessly like this, I felt no tiredness or hunger. From time to time, if I saw a bench or even a convenient wall, I would sit on it, indifferent to the people who would come over to accost me. Baffled by my silence, which led them to assume that I was deaf, they would stand over me, shouting such things as 'You want cigars, cheap cigars, cheap, cheap!' or 'Where you from, mister?' Still I paid them no attention. Then with a shrug, a curse or, on one occasion when the tout was a girl who could not have been more than seven or eight, with the blowing of a raspberry, they wandered off, no doubt to look for some other, more approachable tourist.

Sometimes I would drift into a café or bar. Always I drank the same drink: Havana Club 7 on the rocks. Hadn't Eneas told me that that was the best of all drinks to be found in Cuba? Somehow, by drinking Havana Club 7, I felt, absurdly, that I was keeping faith with Eneas, even if Eneas had broken faith with me.

It was only when, late in the evening, I trudged back to the hotel, that all at once a tidal wave of both exhaustion and hunger swept over me. I was almost too tired to eat and yet I must eat. Fretfully, I called out to the waiter to bring me the menu, to ask why my first course or my second course was taking so long, to demand yet again *'La cuenta! La cuenta!'*

After that I would go up to my room. On one occasion, encountered in the lift, Tel said to me: 'I have two birds up on the roof-terrace. I bargained for only one but the other came along for the ride. Why don't you join us?'

With an effort at politeness, I replied 'Thank you, no. I'm afraid I'm far too tired. It's been a long day.'

Once in my room, I would lie out on the bed, with the air-conditioner mewing away beside me. Immediately I would begin to think of Eneas: of those powerful hands, with the beautifully buffed nails; of those massive legs, thick with hair; of those swelling pectorals, that flat stomach, that cock . . . Then I would reach out for the box of Kleenex tissues which I had placed on the bedside table.

But it was useless. Even in my fantasies, Eneas refused to satisfy me. Tears in my eyes, breathless and giddy from the effort, I would eventually drop off into a sleep lurid with dreams of the skinny black boy flying from rock to rock in the cave, of the police-cars dementedly wailing as they swept up the road, of the beautiful woman officer frowning down at me from her dais, of the young homosexual laughing at me, of everyone in the street laughing at me.

# 19

If Eneas had ever given me his address – and, strangely, I could not be sure – then I had lost it. But fortunately the taxi-driver who had taken me there for the Sunday lunch remembered the way. As we drove out, he talked away in Spanish, from time to time bursting into laughter. That I made absolutely no response, indeed paid absolutely no attention, did not worry him in the least.

In a state of trepidation, I mounted the steps. At my approach the dog had started barking. Now, in a frenzy, she threw herself against the wire mesh. I leaned over, I put out a hand. I was thinking, superstitiously, that it was essential that I placate her, make a friend of her. I was delighted when once again, as in the past, she coiled her long, gluey tongue around my fingers, wagging her huge feather-duster of a tail.

I knocked and waited. I knocked again. Then I began to hammer on the door with my fist. No answer. I stood back from the door and stared at it. I was convinced that behind it there were people – José, the grandparents, perhaps Eneas himself – who were keeping absolutely immobile, absolutely silent, in a determination not to betray their presence.

From his taxi, the driver was watching me. Eventually he called out something in Spanish – probably to tell me that it was useless, there was no one there. I paid no attention to him.

Once again I hammered; and at the din, the dog again began to bark. Sweat was breaking out on my forehead. I could feel a trickle of it snake down my spine.

With a shrug, I at last gave up. I walked down the steps and up the steps of the house next door. That, I remembered, was the house where Alonso lived. Almost as soon as I had rapped peremptorily with the brass knocker shaped like a fish, the door opened. An elderly woman was standing there, supported by a frame made not of metal but, as though by an amateur carpenter, out of bamboo. About her face a check cloth was tied, knotted at the crown, as long ago in England in my childhood cloths used to be tied about the swollen faces of sufferers from toothache. She smiled. She seemed to know who I was. Perhaps she had seen me on one or other of my two visits to Eneas's family.

'Is Alonso here?' She gave me a helpless look.

'Alonso,' I repeated. Then more loudly: '*Alonso.*'

She began to speak very fast. I caught the words '*fuera*', '*lejano*', '*trabajo*'.

'When will he back? *When will he be back?*'

She gabbled something.

Even more loudly I repeated the question.

She recoiled, a sudden look of alarm on her face. Then she stepped away from me, into the house, and slammed the door shut.

Once again the taxi-driver was shouting something in Spanish.

I clambered back into the taxi.

'*Adonde? Adonde?*' the driver now asked.

Where? Where? I had no idea where to go.

'Hotel,' I said.

[177]

# 20

When, groaning, I awoke the next morning, the idea was there, fully formed. It was too early to telephone now at twenty past six. I would wait till after breakfast.

When I did eventually telephone, a woman answered. She could not possibly be Cuban, she must be American or Canadian. When she said that Cesaro was not there, I guessed, I could not have said how, that Cesaro was there but asleep. Later Cesaro himself was to confirm this.

'Can I give him a message? I expect him back, oh, in an hour or two.'

'Please.' I gave her my name. Then I said: 'Please tell him that I'd like to have another Spanish lesson. He knows my hotel. He could ring me here to fix a time.'

'Another Spanish lesson?'

'That's right.' Did she believe me? I wasn't sure.

'Okay. I'll see that he gets your message.'

About forty minutes later, Cesaro rang. The woman must have been within hearing distance, since he was so formal, so obviously careful of what he said. 'You rang, sir? ... I gather that you want another lesson. No problem ... What time did you have in mind?' I wondered how many foreigners rang Cesaro for Spanish lessons. No doubt our mutual friend Rudolf had done so.

At the agreed hour of three o'clock that afternoon, I was waiting for Cesaro in the foyer, with the same mixture of eagerness and apprehension with which I used to wait for Eneas. Unlike Eneas, always at least half an hour late, Cesaro kept me waiting for little more than ten minutes.

'Shall we go up to the roof-terrace?'

To go up to the roof-terrace was clearly Cesaro's way to a client's bedroom without being noticed by any of the staff.

'No, let's have a drink in the downstairs bar. The roof-terrace gets so hot at this time of day. There's something I want to discuss with you. A proposition.'

Cesaro looked puzzled and disconcerted.

Our drinks at last before us – how long even the simplest things took in Cuba! – Cesaro leaned forward and asked: 'So what is this proposition?' Why had he lowered his voice? Apart from the waiter, whose English was confined to taking orders, there was no one else present. It must be habit, I concluded, in a country in which no one trusted anyone.

'I wonder if you could spare me a day? I'd pay you, of course,' I added.

'A *day?*' No doubt Cesaro was thinking, appalled, that I wanted a whole day of sex.

'I need a translator. Someone fluent, like yourself.'

I began to tell him of my plan to go out to the village and to learn what had happened there. I said nothing of Eneas. I merely said that a priest had taken me there for the first time, and that the priest was now no longer in Havana and so it was necessary to look for someone else.

Cesaro scowled as he bit at a thumb-nail. Spitting out the shard of nail, he said: 'I don't like this. This could be dangerous for me. I have heard about what has been happening in that village. It is all a trick of the church.'

'A *trick*?'

'That is what they say. To destabilise the government.' Again he chewed on the thumb-nail. 'I might get into trouble. I must be careful.'

'I'd make it worth your while.'

He pondered, head lowered. Then he looked up and grinned. 'How much?'

'Fifty dollars?'

At once he shook his head. 'Too little.'

'A hundred?' Foolishly, I was not in the mood to bargain.

He pondered. Then, reluctantly, he said: 'Okay.'

'Then we can set off tomorrow? Early. So that we can return the same day.'

He laughed. 'Not too early. I go to bed late, I wake up late.'

'Ten?'

'Okay. But how will we get there?'

'I'll have to hire a taxi.'

Decisively he said: 'I will hire it. I must be careful, I told you. If the taxi-driver talks ... Better a friend of mine.'

'What friend?'

'A taxi-driver friend.'

'All right.'

'It'll be cheaper for you.'

'All right.'

He drained his glass. Then he once again leaned across the table, his voice lowered to almost a whisper: 'Now – shall we go . . .?' A tilt of his head indicated upstairs.

[180]

I shook my head. 'I have to see someone in' – I made a pretence of consulting my watch – 'less than half an hour.'

'Wouldn't you like what Rudolf used to call "a quickie"?'

'I'm no good at quickies. Too old.'

We both laughed. Then he said: 'You are not *so* old.'

'Well, certainly in Cuba I feel at least ten years younger than my age.'

At the door, my curiosity overcoming me, I asked: 'That woman who answered the phone – was she Canadian or American?'

'My girlfriend? Mexican. But she lived in the States for a long, long time. She went to school there – and college there.'

After he had left, I returned to the bar and ordered another drink. I no longer had to say 'Havana Club 7', I merely said 'The usual, please.' Then I began to question myself: Why on earth was I returning to the village? It would probably prove a totally fruitless journey, it might even prove a dangerous one. There was a possibility, certainly, that if nothing had happened to Father Antonio, then he would be able to reveal what had happened to Eneas; and if he could not do that, then he might at least be able to produce Diego's surname and address.

But more than those possibilities had decided me to go. When I had not been thinking about Eneas, I had been thinking about the 'miracle' of the cave. Like Banquo in the case of the witches, I kept asking myself: 'Were such things here as we do speak about? Or have we eaten on the insane root\That takes the reason prisoner?' – except that it was not, in my case, an insane root but a drink of warm, orange-tinged water from a thick glass held out to me by a pallid girl with a hare-lip.

[181]

That someone as materialistic and rational as myself should have had that experience so late in my life was as though I were to pick up the morning newspaper and read 'Scientist proves that sun circles the earth.' There were times when I felt actually giddy with the disorientation I had suffered; and, in a strange way, that disorientation was merely part of another disorientation – that of having fallen in love so totally, so irrationally, so unexpectedly, at so advanced an age.

The barman, no doubt bored, strolled over to me.

'Alone?'

'Yes, alone.'

He gave a sympathetic smile. 'More drink?'

I nodded. Then I said: 'Have one on me.'

'Please?'

I mimed raising a glass and drinking from it and then pointed at the waiter. I took out my wallet and extracted a note.

At last the waiter understood. He grinned. '*Sí! Sí! Gracias, señor!*'

I wondered if the man would really have the drink. No doubt, like most barmen in such circumstances, he would decide to keep the money instead.

# 21

Cesaro told me that the driver was called Juan – 'He is a good friend of mine. We were neighbours. We went to the same school. Sometimes we even had the same girlfriends.' Speaking no English, Juan grinned. Was Cesaro lying? It seemed impossible that the two men, one with his thinning, obviously dyed hair and the other with his youthfully perky face under a baseball cap worn back to front, should be the same age.

As we got into the car, Cesaro asked: 'Do you like Juan's shorts?'

Baggy and reaching well below the knees, the shorts were printed over, green on red, with large maple leaves.

'Very smart.'

Cesaro translated my comment. Then he said: 'A Canadian tourist gave them to him.'

Why should a Canadian tourist have given Juan the shorts? Were the boy not so skinny and plain, I might have suspected a liaison.

'Haven't you got some shorts like that to give me?'

'I don't wear shorts. Old men's legs are far from attractive.'

'You should tell that to the Canadians!'

At Cesaro's suggestion, we first stopped at the diplomatic store to lay in provisions for the journey. Totally familiar with the layout, Cesaro marched me to each counter and then imperiously indicated what I should buy: Beer, mineral water, two bottles of hugely expensive Muscadet from the cold cabinet, ham, bread, butter, cheese . . . The purchases went on and on.

'We'll never get through all this,' I eventually protested.

'Never mind.' Cesaro gave a saucy smile. 'Juan and I can take home what is left. If I take home some nice things this evening, my girlfriend won't worry so much about the Spanish lesson going on for so long.'

For most of the journey I slept or half-slept, while Juan and Cesaro, seated side by side, kept up an endless chatter. Juan's voice was particularly loud and shrill and his laughter, which erupted frequently, sounded like a saw ripping through ply-wood. I wished that they would shut up, but did not feel that I could tell them to do so.

On this occasion the village was almost deserted. An old, bowed man, limping along, gnarled stick in gnarled hand, paused and stared, as the woman with the cockerel had paused and stared on the previous occasion. Two tiny children, seeing the car, began to run after it in pursuit, perhaps in the hope of a coin or a sweet; then realising the impossibility of keeping up, they faltered and fell back. A mangy dog, asleep in the middle of the road, bestirred itself lethargically at the sound of the horn, and limped out of the way. I thought, with a pang of disquet, of the mystery of that huge dog rushing out on the previous occasion, and hurling himself to his death under the wheels.

There were a number of other dogs in the square, all of them asleep in the heat of the early afternoon. Perhaps the inhabitants were also asleep. It was not surprising that all the shops should be closed, since that was now a commonplace in Cuba; but it was surprising that people were not lounging around, chatting to each other, or listening to sport on the radio, or simply doing nothing, since that too was now a commonplace.

The girl with the hare-lip – she seemed much more attractive, with her high cheekbones and her translucent complexion and her large, dark eyes, than I had remembered – opened the door. By now Cesaro and I were by ourselves. Juan was in the car, all its doors open because of the heat, sleeping or trying to sleep. At the sight of us, an expression of alarm replaced the smile which the girl had had ready for whoever was calling. She took a step back, then called over her shoulder, on a note of rising panic: '*Padre! Padre!*'

His face and hands that weird colour, silver blotched with verdigris, Father Antonio eventually shuffled out from the room which on the previous visit he had pointed out as his. He was no longer in clerical garb but in pyjamas, with a faded and worn plaid shawl thrown over his bony shoulders.

He seemed totally unsurprised to see me; but at the same time he did nothing to welcome me, standing there still and silent, his huge eyes, set deep in their sockets, fixed on my face with a tranquil sadness of expression.

Cesaro was briskly efficient. Before I could say anything, he had announced who he was and had then, uninvited, stepped into the house, followed by me. Father Antonio pointed down the corridor, to the little sitting-room.

As soon as we were seated, Cesaro turned to me: 'Now what is it that you want to ask him?' Clearly he had no intention of wasting time.

[185]

'Well, first I want to know if there has been any more trouble from the police.'

In that high-pitched voice of his, the words constantly stumbling and expiring, Father Antonio began to give his answer. From time to time Cesaro repeated something, as though he wanted confirmation of it; from time to time he asked a question to clarify this or that; from time to time he turned to me to translate. The priest's lips were dry and cracked, and there were sores, like small nicks, at each corner of them. The tip of his tongue tentatively explored one of these sores whenever, head on one side, he was deliberating what to answer.

Yes, Father Antonio said, the police had been back. They had questioned him, questioned him repeatedly, asking the same questions which they had asked the previous time and receiving the same answers from him. Then, he added with a sigh, they had threatened him. But – what did he care? He was far too old and ill to care.

How had they threatened him? Cesaro translated my question.

Oh, they had told him that, if he wasn't careful, he would find himself in prison. Well, he'd been in that prison once before, he had almost died in it. Things couldn't be any worse this time than they were then.

Ask him about the children, the three children, I told Cesaro.

The question put to him, the old man leaned his head back and closed his eyes. There was nothing to support the head, as he sat upright on the wooden chair. The posture looked terribly uncomfortable. He gave a groan, followed by another. I thought: Oh God, he's been taken ill! But then the priest opened his eyes. He began to talk.

Two women had come with the police. They called themselves social workers but, if they were indeed social workers, then they and the police must work hand in hand. The women questioned the children here, in this house, in this very room. They questioned them on and on, for three, four hours. Their parents were not allowed to be present, he himself was not allowed to be present. It was easy to see that the children were terrified. From his bedroom he had been able to hear one of the girls sobbing.

After the inquisitions the two women had announced that the children were 'profoundly disturbed' – that was the phrase used by Cesaro in translating to me. They needed help, treatment, expert treatment. They would have to go to be treated in a special clinic for children, now, at once.

There had been a terrible scene when the children were driven away in a mini-bus specially sent for them. They had screamed and fought. The boy had almost escaped, racing up the hill behind the house where he lived with his aunt and uncle. Having recaptured him, the police had then tied him up, squealing, kicking and biting. Like a chicken trussed for the market, Cesaro translated. Almost everyone in the village had turned up in angry protest. But the police had ordered them back to their homes, threatening them with prison if they did not obey.

Where was the clinic to which the children had been taken? I asked.

Cesaro again translated.

An evasive look appeared on the old man's face. He shrugged, pulled at one end of the shawl, adjusted it over his bony shoulders. He did not know, he said.

'But he must have some idea,' I told Cesaro.

'I think that for some reason he doesn't want you to know.'

[187]

'But why? Why?'

'In Cuba people who try to make things better usually make them only worse. That's particularly true of foreigners.'

'Are they in Havana?'

Cesaro translated the old man's answer: 'Perhaps.'

'Perhaps?'

I looked at Father Antonio and the priest then gave me a little shrug and the spectre of a smile. Once again he began to fidget with the shawl.

'I'd have liked to visit them. To find out what exactly is going on.'

Cesaro made no attempt to translate this.

'Please tell him that.'

Reluctantly Cesaro translated. Then, having listened to the answer, head on one side, he told me: 'He says that is not a good idea. If you tried to help them, you would only harm them more. You are a foreigner. It is better if you do not interest yourself.'

During all this, his eyes fixed on my face, while the tip of his tongue flickered at one corner of his mouth, the old man kept nodding.

'Is there anything else you want me to ask him?'

'Yes. Does he know what happened to Eneas?'

'Eneas?'

'Yes.'

'Who is this Eneas?'

'Someone who was here at the same time as my priest friend and I. Ask him, please.'

'What is his surname?'

Reluctantly I told him: 'De León.'

'He knows little about this Eneas De León. There was a rumour . . .'

'What rumour?'

Again Cesarò turned to Father Antonio. Then he told me: 'There was a rumour that he was in trouble. Someone, a policeman, recognised him, or someone here reported him. No one knows for sure.'

'What kind of trouble?'

Cesaro now translated: 'He does not know. Some say one thing, some another. Prison maybe.'

'*Prison?*'

'He does not really know. These are only rumours, talk . . . Is this Eneas a policeman?'

Since Father Antonio must have already revealed that he was, there was no point in denying it. 'Yes.'

'And he is your friend?'

'I met him here. He's related to the priest I mentioned.'

'I see.'

A silence followed. Then Cesaro prompted me: 'Is there anything else?'

I hesitated. Then I said: 'Yes. Ask him – ask him if he believes that what took place in the cave was really a miracle?'

Father Antonio stared at me in incredulity, his red-rimmed eyes wide. Then he threw back his head and burst into a shrill whinny of laughter. Tears of mirth began to form along his lower lids.

Cesaro shrugged. 'I think you have your answer. He believes. These country people believe anything, anything.'

When there was clearly nothing more to be learned from Father Antonio, I told Cesaro that perhaps we had better set off on our journey home. I was thinking of the cost of the taxi.

Cesaro got up from his chair, stretching and yawning. 'Villages like this are full of superstition. Time passes, governments change. But everything in these villages is always the same. Miracles, magic.' He smiled at me and then smiled at Father Antonio. 'They are not really Christians,' he said. 'Theirs is the religion of Africa.'

I was hardly listening. My mind was besieged with thoughts of Eneas. Was he really in prison? Was that possible? And if he was, how would I ever get news of him, how would I ever see him again?

Before our departure, I walked down the narrow, murky passage to the lavatory. As I passed the room in which Eneas and I had spent the night together, I suddenly, on an impulse, turned the handle and opened the door. I stared at the bed. That was where we had lain in each other's arms. That was where I had tried to kiss him on the mouth and he had repulsed me.

That was where he had had his convulsive orgasm, his body shuddering as though in a violent fever. A small miracle had taken place in that room, just as a huge miracle had taken place in the cave; and that small miracle had been the consequence of another one, also small – that extraordinary access of energy and youthfulness and joy which I had experienced ever since my arrival in this country. I crossed to the bed and placed a hand on the long, hard bolster at its head. I ran the hand up and down, up and down.

Then, suddenly, I heard a sound behind me. It was the girl. When I turned round, she was scowling at me with a mixture of amazement and outrage. This was the room she shared with her mother. She must be wondering why on earth I was there and what I was doing.

I gave her a taut smile, pushed past her and continued on up the corridor.

\*

It was only after I had taken Father Antonio's narrow, bony, dry hand in mine in farewell, that I thought of the last question which I had wished to put to him: Did the old priest know where I could find Diego, Father Diego?

Father Antonio paused, muttered something, began to shake his head. Then he turned away and shuffled back into the house.

'Is he coming back?'

Cesaro shrugged.

Eventually, Father Antonio shuffled out again. He held out a piece of paper, a scrap torn off a newspaper. He had scribbled something on it in a faint, spidery hand. It was Diego's full name and an address in Havana.


'So what do I owe him?'

Cesaro turned to Juan, who was using a feather-duster to brush some biscuit crumbs off the back seat of the car. 'I will ask.' After some discussion in low voices in Spanish, he told me: 'Two-fifty dollars.'

'What?'

'The village is far away. We left early and now it is late.'

'Even so . . .'

'Gas is very expensive. He had to buy it on the black market.'

'But this is a licensed taxi, a dollar taxi. Surely he gets petrol for his work?'

'For driving in Havana. Not for a journey to the country.'

'If I give him as much as that, my dollars won't last me out. I've used up my traveller's cheques. And I have to find a hundred dollars for you,' I added, suddenly remembering.

[191]

The two men again conferred in low voices in Spanish. Then Cesaro said: 'Have you got credit cards?'

'Yes. Why?'

'Well, Juan suggests that we go back to the diplomatic store and you can buy him some things there. For two hundred and fifty dollars. And, if it is more convenient for you, you can buy some things for me. For one hundred dollars. Okay?'

I sighed. 'Okay.'


When the taxi had once more returned me to the hotel, Cesaro asked in a wheedling voice: 'Juan and I can take the food we didn't eat?' He pointed to the two carrier bags on the back seat. When I hesitated, not because I wanted the food but because the two Cubans had so blatantly ripped me off, Cesaro reminded me: 'You promised.'

'Did I? . . . Yes, take them, take them.'

'You are a real English gentleman!'

At that he threw his arms around me and kissed me first on one cheek and then on the other.

## 22

I began to feel nervous as, constantly looking at my map, I wandered down one squalid street and then one even more squalid. At least the streets of Old Havana were beautiful, even though so many of their once grandiose mansions were now on the verge of collapse. But here, in this suburb, there was nothing to please or placate the eye. In the late nineteenth century when these buildings had been erected, the poor had lived in them; and now the poor continued to do so.

Few of the streets were named and few of the houses were numbered. When I stopped a passerby, educated-looking and reasonably well-dressed, and showed him a street on my map for confirmation, he shook his head crossly and, without a word, strode on. No one in Cuba had ever before treated me like that, I might have been in Paris or New York.

I thought that I had been more fortunate with a young woman, pushing an ancient buggy with a pop-eyed child in it. But whether because she genuinely did not know the way or because she took a malicious pleasure in misleading a foreigner, she sent me, I discovered after many minutes of walking, in precisely the opposite direction. Why had I not asked Cesaro to accompany me, however exorbitant the cost? Why, at least, had I not hired a taxi, instead of tramping for all this time through these baking, stinking streets?

At last I came on the house. The two spindly columns on either side of its steps had once held up a portico; but the portico must have collapsed, since there was no sign of it now. The steps themselves were crumbling, with weeds growing out of their fissures. Could Diego really be living in such a slum? He had shown none of the signs of malnutrition so common in the country, and he had looked so prosperous – his feet shod in leather, his watch an expensive Seiko one, a gold chain with a crucifix dangling round his neck.

The hall was so gloomy that, coming in from the glare of the street, I had to wait, even after I had pulled off my dark glasses, for my eyes to accustom themselves. There were three shut doors and one, the nearest, ajar. I went over to the door which was ajar and knocked on it. A female voice called out. Hesitatingly, I entered.

In a soiled towelling bathrobe, her hennaed hair dishevelled, a woman was seated, her feet in mules with bedraggled feathers on them, at an antiquated treadle sewing-machine beside the window. Perched on the window ledge was what I took to be a wizened dwarf, hunched over as if in pain, her arms around her stomach. Then, when she jumped down from the window ledge, I realised that this was in fact a small girl.

I smiled and said Diego's name.

The woman looked alarmed; the child retreated behind the chair on which the woman was sitting. Probably I was the first foreigner who had ever entered their room. Perhaps I was the first foreigner who had ever addressed either of them.

[194]

I held out the scrap of paper on which Father Antonio had written the name and address.

The woman took it from me and, mouth bunched, peered at it for a long time. Perhaps she could not read, I thought – even though Tel, enumerating all the blessings of the Castro regime, had placed universal education at the top of them. She drew in her lower lip, she frowned, she sighed. Then she handed the scrap of paper not to me but to the girl, saying something to her.

The girl ran out from behind the chair and pushed past me through the door and out into the corridor. She turned her head and made a hissing sound at me. The woman raised a hand and flapped it back and forth – I was to follow the girl, I gathered.

The small, bare, grubby feet raced up the cracked stone steps to the first landing. An immensely fat woman, her face heavily seamed and her hair in paper curlers, was lying there, fanning herself with a newspaper, on a wicker *chaise-longue*. The girl paused, waiting for me. Indicating me with her newspaper, the woman must have asked who I was. The girl shrugged and gave a high-pitched giggle. The woman stared at me and finally said: *'Buenos días'*, in a breathless, slurred voice.

Up and up we climbed, the girl scurrying ahead and then waiting at each landing, while I, hand to banister – later I was to discover my palm grey with dust – panted up behind her. At the very top, where there had once been a skylight but where there was now merely an empty square stuffed with newspaper, she called out 'Padre Diego!' and I heard a muffled voice answering.

She turned the handle of the door against which she was leaning. *'Vaya!'* Then she held out her hand. It was all too clear what she expected.

I felt in the breast pocket of my jacket for one of the

one-dollar notes that I kept there for tips. I plucked it out and proffered it.

With a shrill yelp of delight she snatched it from me. Once again pushing past me, she began to race down the stairs, screaming out something as she did so. No doubt she was telling her mother of her good fortune.

Diego lay on a narrow, iron bed, under a window from which it was barely possible to see out, so caked was it with grime. The room was small, low-ceilinged, with nothing else in it but a large table, scattered with books, a wardrobe perilously tilting, two straightbacked chairs and, amazingly in such squalor, what looked like a brand-new television set. Beside the television set, on the floor, were the shoes which he had worn to the village, a pair of jeans, a tee-shirt. A bottle of rum was also on the floor, by the bed.

He was cocooned, on this day of extravagant heat, in a blanket which almost totally covered his head. His knees were drawn up, his face – what I could see of it – was unshaven, blotched and sweaty. He was shivering uncontrollably. He gazed at me with bloodshot eyes. Then he rasped, with a mixture of annoyance and amazement: 'Why – why the hell . . .?'

I was still panting after my climb. 'I'm sorry. But I couldn't telephone. And I thought that, if I sent a letter, it'd probably never reach you.'

'A visit is the last thing I need.' With a groan, he threw back the blanket and, still shivering, sat up on the bed. He was wearing only a pair of Y-fronts. His whole, hairy body was glistening with sweat.

'Are you ill?'

'Malaria . . . Ever since I was in Africa . . .' He broke off, convulsed by another shudder.

[196]

I looked around me, still breathless and overcome by the rancid stink. Then gradually, my joints still stiff from that climb up to the cave, I lowered myself into one of the chairs.

Balefully, Diego stared at me, pearls of sweat trickling down the hollow between his hairy breasts.

I cleared my throat. 'Can I do anything for you?'

A bark of contemptuous laughter jerked out of him. He shook his head. 'No, nothing. Nothing, kind Englishman.' Again he gave me that baleful stare. 'It'll pass. Tomorrow or the day after tomorrow. It always does. Meanwhile – I feel like hell.'

'Is someone . . . seeing to things for you?'

'Seeing to things?' Diego put the words into mocking inverted commas. 'Oh, yes, from to time to time the neighbours . . . We're a very neighbourly lot in this slum of ours.' With another groan, he toppled back on to the bed, rolled over, drew his legs up, once more hitched the blanket around him. 'I don't imagine you came here to ask after my well-being. Did you?'

'No. I'd no idea you were ill.'

'Of course not! How could you have any idea?' His teeth were chattering. Presumably to stop the chattering, he put up a hand and gripped his jaw. 'So – why are you here?'

'It's about Eneas. I thought you might be able to tell me how to find him.' When there was no response to this, I pushed on: 'He seems to have – vanished.'

'Yes . . . Vanished.' Diego rolled over on to his back and stared up at the ceiling. Suddenly, disconcertingly, he began to hum to himself, tonelessly, on two or three repeated notes.

'Do you know where he is?'

[197]

He did not answer, continuing to hum. Far off I could hear the siren of a police-car, suddenly reminding me of those police-cars roaring up the road to the cave.

'Diego . . .?'

'Yes, I think I know. But really . . . really . . . I do honestly believe it to be better not to tell you.'

'I don't understand.'

'Don't you? Well, that hardly surprises me. But I do honestly believe . . . Certainly better for him, perhaps better for you.'

I now wanted only to leave him and his stinking room. But doggedly I persisted: 'Is he in prison?'

'Not exactly.' There was a long pause. 'But . . . He's in trouble, big trouble.'

'Because of our journey, you mean?'

'Partly. And because of other things. He's been a silly boy. A brave boy but a silly boy.'

I moved over to the bed. In a sudden fury of impatience, I resisted the impulse to put out a hand to his shoulder and shake him. 'You must tell me how I can help him.' Once more he had set up that tuneless humming. 'Please!'

'The best way for you to help him is to do nothing at all. To leave him alone. To – forget him.' The blanket held with one hand under his stubbly chin, his teeth had again begun to chatter – so violently that I could hear their staccato rat-tat-tat against each other.

'I don't get you. Why? Why?'

'Any foreigner of any kind would only make things worse.' It was what Cesaro and Father Antonio had also said. Diego tilted his head and squinted up at me. 'As for a silly old foreign queen . . .'

It was as though I had suddenly received a punch in the face. I recoiled, almost lost my balance. Then, eyes

[198]

blinking, with a pathetic attempt at defiance and dignity I countered: 'I don't see why even a silly old foreign queen might not be able to do something.'

'Don't you?' The tone was vicious. 'Well, the problem is that there are some things that even your dollars can't buy. Food, drink, clothes, a camera, yes – immunity for your Cuban pals, no.' Suddenly he jumped off the bed, the blanket held up to his chin with his left hand, while with his right he grasped the lapels of my jacket, twisting them tight. He began to shake me. 'Don't you understand, you stupid, senile old fool? Don't you understand anything? When governments are threatened with extinction, they grow paranoid.' His voice was hoarse, his face was close to mine, his breath fetid. 'They suspect all kinds of plots – internal plots, yes, but even more, foreign plots. If you concern yourself with Eneas, then perhaps you'll be the next . . . Oh, what the hell!' Releasing me, he gave me a shove so violent that I all but fell over.

'So I must do nothing? Is that what you think?' Suddenly, I felt a terrible pain in the centre of my chest, as though a knife had pierced it. Was I having a heart attack? I found myself gasping for breath, the sweat breaking out on my body.

Diego sank back on to the bed again. 'Precisely. Nothing. Nothing at all. Got it? If you wish to help him, you'll go away, leave Cuba, not try to get in touch with him, or with his family, or with me, or with anyone. That's the best thing you can do for all of us. That's the best thing you can do for yourself.'

'But I can't . . .' Helplessly I looked down at him. 'How can I? Eneas is . . .'

'Oh, Christ!' Then, amazingly, he softened. 'I know, I know. I know all about that.' With a groan he raised his body, tilted it forward, was eventually once more sitting

[199]

on the edge of the bed. He crossed his hairy legs at the ankles. He bowed his head and put his hands, fingers interlinked, across the nape of it. 'But what you must understand is that what you feel for him is not what he feels for you, not at all, not at all. Don't you understand that?' He jerked his head up; then let it tip sideways, as though it were too heavy for the neck. The bleary, bloodshot eyes were staring, askew, at me. 'Don't you?'

'Yes . . . Of course.'

'He's fond of you, of course he's fond of you. He's grateful to you. But don't suppose . . . I know Eneas well. Probably better even than his mother ever did. When he was a young boy, sixteen, seventeen . . .' He smiled in recollection, his face all at once suffused with a melting tenderness.

'Yes?'

He shrugged. Then he jerked his body round, to gaze out towards the grimy window. I knew then, knew with total certainty, that, like myself now, he had once been in love with Eneas. Perhaps he still was.

'I'm sorry. I'm sorry for you. I truly am. The fact is . . . the fact is . . . you shouldn't have come to Cuba. No one should come to Cuba.'

'Oh, I'm glad I came. I don't regret it . . . I'll never regret it.'

For a long time, head still tilted to one side, he continued to stare out towards the window. Then he raised an arm before his face, as though to ward off some invisible blow. 'Oh, beat it! Go on! Beat it! I'm too ill to bother with you.' His voice was hoarse. He was closing his eyes.

I still stood by the bed. 'Can't I do anything?'

'No.' Then he opened his eyes wide and yelled it. 'No!'

Once out of the room I began to race down the stairs.

[200]

# 23

All one night I looked for them, with the same obsessive determination with which I had once looked for Eneas. I threaded the park, back and forth and round and round. I trailed up to the Plaza de Armas. I wandered along the sea-front, even though Raul had given me that warning that at night it was often the scene of muggings. I felt no tiredness, I felt no thirst. Then, as the dawn was breaking, I returned to the hotel, fell fully clothed on to my bed, and experienced a sleep which was a kind of protracted dying.

On the second night, the night before my departure, I all at once saw the ancient car, its skin like that of a bruised pear, parked just beyond the Hotel Nacional. For a while I stood by it; then I leaned against it, from time to time kicking at its nearest tyre, its tread perilously worn away.

After a long time – half an hour, three quarters of an hour – I at last saw them emerging from the hotel and, arm in arm, swaying towards me up the wide, gravel drive. They were close to one another, their bodies from time to time colliding. There was a wind off the sea that night and it lifted the hem of her dress and ruffled his hair. They were laughing together at something .

Eventually seeing me, they quickened their pace. They smiled at me.

'May we help you?' the man said.

*Yes, yes! I want another miracle. Not a miracle as momentous as that scene in the cave, or as that love-making on that hard, creaking bedstead. I don't now want you to give me those old feelings of excitement, energy, exhilaration, passion, pleasure, amazement. I want only one thing. Peace. I want you to give me peace. That's all. Peace.*

The man had opened the door of the car beside me. He said: 'Get in.' Now it was he who sat beside me, and she who sat in front.

The man twisted his slim, supple body round to face me. 'A hundred,' he said.

'A hundred dollars?'

The man nodded.

'But last time . . .'

'These things become more expensive.' He raised his eyebrows, he smiled.

The woman had turned to lean over to me from the seat in front. 'A hundred,' she said. She too now smiled.

'But I haven't got a hundred dollars.' Of all the many dollars that I had brought out to Cuba, I now had only twenty-seven left.

'Too bad.' Probably they did not believe me.

'Twenty-five,' I pleaded.

'Sorry.'

'*Please!*'

'Sorry!' The man's voice was harsh.

'But I must . . .'

With a violent thrust of his body against mine, the man leaned over to push down the latch of the car door and open it. Then he shoved with both hands, and I was

[202]

toppling out into the road. I fell on to my back, a gigantic cockroach, its limbs in the air.

I heard the engine starting up. I heard the woman's laughter, strangely distorted, as though it were coming from a radio not properly tuned in. Then the ancient car lumbered off.

A moment after that I felt the agonising kick at my ribs and, another moment after that, the hand clawing at my watch-strap.

# 24

Fortunately the plane was far from full, so that, at its back, they had been able to give me three seats on which to stretch out.

The middle-aged Cuban steward, with the strong, serene face and the luxuriant hair swept back over his ears, was extraordinarily kind. 'What happened?' he asked in a gentle, awed voice, as he covered my body with a rug. 'A car accident?'

'No, a bicycle one. A bicycle ran into me. I wasn't looking where I was going.' A bicycle accident seemed more likely than a car one in the streets of Havana. For some reason still obscure to me even today, I did not wish to tell him that I had been mugged.

'You should have been more careful.'

'Yes, I know.'

The steward repeatedly came over to ask me 'Are you all right?' Later, having set down a dinner tray for me, he squatted beside me, to enquire in that same gentle, awed voice: 'Would you like me to feed you?' I shook my head, managing a smile. 'Actually, I don't want anything to eat.' The steward made a tut-tutting sound, as one might to a child. Then he said: 'You must eat. We do not reach Stanstead for more than seven hours.'

Just as, when a small child, I used to force myself to eat when I had no appetite, in order to please my mother, so now I forced myself to eat some of the chill meat and limp salad in order to please the steward. But after a few mouthfuls of food – each had been difficult to swallow – I gave up. I reached over for my glass of Havana Club 7 and sipped and sipped again. Then I began to think of Eneas.

In a sense I had known him completely, since there was no part of his body that I could not remember in every detail: the mole on his left arm, just above the elbow; the way in which one of his little toes overlapped the toe next to it; the thick chest-hair which sprouted at the collar of his tee-shirt; the curve of his buttocks; the upward tilt of his uncut cock when he was lying on the bed beside me . . .

But of Eneas, as distinct from Eneas's body, what did I know? He was boisterous, vain, sunny, childish, brave, honest, inconsiderate. Yes, he was all those things. But there was so much else at which I could only guess. Why had he sought out my company and then devoted so much time to me? The cynical explanation could only be that his family were living near to starvation and that I was a foreigner with dollars and therefore with access to shops which they could never use. But, unlike so many other Cubans, he had never once asked me for anything; and when I had given him anything, he had always either protested indignantly or become sullen with embarrassment and shame.

And why that night had it been he who had taken me in his arms and not the other way about? He was not homosexual, I could not deceive myself into thinking him to be homosexual. But surely, in some way, he must have loved me. *Surely.*

Once again the steward approached. Solicitously, he bent over me. 'Don't you want to eat any more?'

I shook my head, wincing as I raised my arm to hand the steward the tray.

'You've eaten very little.'

'Yes ... Sorry.'

'Would you like something else?'

'No, no. Thank you. I'm just not hungry.'

'Why don't you try to sleep? I could fetch you two aspirins.'

'No, no. Thank you. I'll be fine.'

Somehow I wanted the physical pain, because it distracted me from that other, far more terrible pain within me.

Later, however, when the two pains had become almost intolerable, I thought of the tablets which the doctor at the Clinic for Foreign Patients in Havana had given to me. I had no idea what they were but clearly they were powerful. I fumbled for the bottle in my trouser pocket and eventually, without water, swallowed two of the large, round, flat discs. Soon after that I had fallen asleep.

... I was in the cave once again; but on this occasion, except for Eneas, it was totally empty. I looked up at a ledge of rock, glistening with moisture above me, and then, on an instant, effortlessly – *I can do it, I can do it!* – I had flown up to it. Eneas burst into laughter, he raised his hands and clapped. I looked down at him, then looked up to a ledge even higher. Effortlessly again, I flew up to it too. Up and up I soared, in triumphant ecstasy, while Eneas, standing below, watched, head uptilted. From time to time, I cried out: 'Eneas, look!

Look!' From time to time he again clapped his hands, or laughed in joyful amazement, or shouted 'Bravo!'

Then I began my descent, fluttering from one ledge to another, my feet landing unerringly now on some shelf, now on some sharp pinnacle of rock. Eneas was holding out his arms: 'Come! Come! Come!' he called in encouragement. I felt a wild joy. *I am flying! I am free! A miracle!*

Then, all at once, inexplicably, terrifyingly, my feet were slipping on the humped, bald surface of the rock on which I had just alighted. I put out a hand to clutch at a rock nearby. My body tilted sideways. Then I was falling, falling, falling. As I fell, I let out a piercing, protracted scream . . .

. . . Sweating, shivering, I awoke. I muttered. 'Oh, God, God, God!' Without my stolen watch, I could only wonder for how long I had been sleeping. It seemed a long, long time.

Eyes once more shut, I began yet again to wonder where Eneas was, and what precisely he had done, and what would happen to him. Was he in trouble merely because he had gone to the cave? Or had he actually plotted against the regime? Had they sacked him, imprisoned him, tortured him, executed him?

Again, as during my visit to Diego, I felt that pain in the centre of my chest, as though a knife had pierced it. Again I was disagreeably aware of the sweat breaking out on my body and had to gulp for breath.

The questions jangled in my mind, so many deafening, dissonant bells, as they continue to jangle, on and on, on and on.

There are never any answers to them.

# 25

My two actor neighbours, Tom and Dave, will no doubt see (since they see everything) the inconspicuous little Volkswagen drawing up and the young black man in the shabby brown suit getting out of it and hurrying up my steps. 'Look what he's got for himself!' one of them will call out to the other. 'Not bad,' the other will say, peering round the window frame. 'Rent of course.'

Later, when I next run into them, as I so often do, in the Oxfam shop or at Marks and Spencer or at the pub on the corner, one of the two will probably remark: 'Well, that was an attractive visitor you had, I must say!'

*Surprise me!*

But I will not surprise them.

I will not tell them of that costly, fine ash that my visitor, first met in a Notting Hill Gate pub, brings to my house. I will not speak of the small miracle, that temporary assuagement, or that illusion of a temporary assuagement, that the ash works for me.

I will merely say: 'Yes, he *was* rather dishy, wasn't he?'